AF273155

Diane Jo

The Good,
The Bad and
The Unwanted

novum 📖 pocket

© 2024 novum publishing

ISBN 978-3-903468-46-7
Cover photo:
Esther19775 I Dreamstime.com
Cover design, layout & typesetting:
novum publishing

www.novum-publishing.co.uk

Print product with financial
climate contribution
ClimatePartner.com/16547-2311-1001

Dedicated to my dear late father ' Ernie'
who was "grandad" to all of the children
I have fostered over the years.
He would never have understood this story
because he only knew about giving love
and kindness but he had been very proud
that it was to be published.

Contents

PREFACE

I wrote this short novel based on some experiences during my vast and extensive career as a child protection social worker.

Some of the quotes are verbatim, taken from things which children have said to me over the years.

Some of the characters are based on children and people I have worked alongside – positively or otherwise!

The underlying message of course is how things can go badly wrong for children who are not loved unconditionally, who do not form positive attachments, who are not wanted, and how the system can fail them, and they become labelled 'bad'.

The story is, of course, fictional and dramatised.

Any quotes from research are included under 'fair use' and the poetry is my own.

Despite being fictional, nothing has shaped my thinking more than listening to and working with other social workers, foster carers, adoptive carers, and disadvantaged parents, but most of all my thinking has been shaped from working endlessly with abused, neglected, and unwanted children.

I hope for my audience to be:

Social workers – who will go on to look beyond the surface and bring 'professional curiosity' into their daily practice.

Foster carers and adoptive parents – to always question their desire and reasons for helping and caring for other people's children. So many of them do it lovingly and unconditionally – but not all!

Parents – who want to look after their children better than they do but don't know where to go for help.

But mostly, I want my audience to be anyone out there who knew neglect and abuse as a child and then became labelled 'bad'. You are not!

Everyone deserves to be loved and wanted.

THE LONELY REFLECTION
(By Diana Jo)

As I looked in the mirror through childhood,
I saw a reflection of me
Unwanted, unloved and uncared for,
which was not what I wanted to see.
I grew and the mirror grew with me,
but each time I looked was the same,
A child staring back with the saddest of eyes,
full of longing and needing and shame.
As an adult I still have a mirror,
and I look in it most days to see
The same reflection I saw as a child,
a lonely, unlovable me.
I am going to change my reflection;
I am going to set myself free,
When I've learned that its okay to just love myself,
the mirror will change just like me.

PROLOGUE

Nobody is born bad, but some people are born unwanted.
  'A silent cry, a hungry child, emotions that are stunted,
  When I was born, I was not bad, but I knew I was
unwanted.'

Leo was born on Halloween, and as he grew up, he often wondered whether this was the reason for the good and the bad in him.

Leo was born and raised not knowing who his father was.

As he grew older, he questioned whether his mother knew, but she was always ambivalent about this.

'Just a bloke, for God's sake, Leo. How am I supposed to know?'

Leo was about six when he realised that his mum was a sex worker, although he never really understood the 'label' which people gave her, or what a 'label' was: 'prostitute, hooker, whore.'

He knew the men came and went, he knew there were noises and grunts from his mum's bedroom when the men were there, and she always had money afterwards.

Leo was seven when the police came one night. He had been lying under his thin blanket in bed. He could hear his mum's screams and pleas for things to stop. He knew she was being beaten and hurt in other ways although he couldn't really understand.

He knew he was scared; he was picking at the skin on his hands again as he tried to not listen. He knew his hands would be raw in the morning as he picked at them furiously.

He knew his mum would be bruised again; 'black and blue', that's what he had heard it called.

He knew she would cover herself in make-up. He *hated* that make-up so much. He wished he could throw it all in the bin.

If she didn't have the make-up to cover the bruises, then she might stop getting the bruises, he thought.

Leo's thoughts started to get fuzzy. He was so tired. He hadn't had any tea tonight because mum was being a 'prostitute, a whore, a hooker'!

He pleaded to himself for the screaming and the sounds of thuds and grunting to stop but they didn't stop. They carried on, and he knew his mum would be all cut and bleeding again; he just knew it.

Then came the KNOCK!

The knock on the door which changed everything that night. Leo's life was never going to be the same again.

'POLICE HERE! LET US IN, NOW!' The screaming stopped, the thuds stopped, the grunting stopped.

Someone let the police in, he can't remember who – maybe they forced their way in like in the films he had watched a few times when the men weren't here and mum was nice.

He remembers the police lady who came into his bedroom – well, his mum called it a bedroom. He had heard the social workers say that it was not appropriate. It was basically a cupboard under the stairs, but nonetheless it was where he slept night after night, cold, sometimes hungry, listening to his mum being 'a prostitute, a whore, a hooker', or whatever she was when the men came and went.

The police lady was kind, he thinks. She had a round face and was smiling as she came toward him.

'Well then, what have we here? What's your name, little fella?'

Leo had hidden under his blanket. His mum had told him all about the police and social workers. They didn't help; they made it worse. He tried to remember what his mum had told him to say.

She was closer now, the smiley police lady. She edged toward Leo's bed and said, 'Don't be scared. We are here to help.'

He couldn't remember kind words like this since his grandma had died. Something inside snapped and he started to cry, really cry, and tremble, and scream.

He couldn't stop, he just couldn't stop. He knew he was startling the police lady, but he couldn't stop.

'SARGE!' shouted the police officer. 'Come in here, Sarge, you need to see this.'

'I think we will need police protection. There's a child here – he's terrified, he looks half-starved. Please, Sarge, come here.'

As the bulky sergeant came and stood in the cupboard doorway, there was no room left. Leo thought it was like a cartoon where everyone was big and the surroundings were small. It was comical, but he still kept screaming.

'Boody hell,' said the sergeant. 'What the fuck? The poor little bugger. Call Children's Services, Officer. Do it now, right away. He can't stay here.'

Just as Leo was wondering what would happen to him next, he saw another police officer leading a man out of his mum's bedroom. The man wasn't resisting. He was half-dressed, head down and muttering 'obscenities' (Leo thought that was the grown-up word for swearing, anyway).

'Fuckin' bitch. More trouble than she's worth, bloody big mouth screaming and crying. She got what she deserved. She would have soon taken my money.'

Behind the man, Leo could see his mum. A different police lady was trying to help her get dressed. She was *really* black and blue. She looked as if she were broken in two. She couldn't stand up; she was doubled over.

Leo felt his heart pounding. He wanted to go to her, to help her. He would even put the make-up on for her if it would help.

His mum looked at him through bloodshot eyes. He didn't recognise his own emotions as pity and concern. He tried to smile at her.

Sometimes, very rarely, when the men weren't around, they smiled at each other, and he would feel warm and nice inside afterwards.

Leo heard the sergeant say, 'We are taking him into protective custody, madam. Would you like to say goodbye?'

Leo froze. What was protective custody? What did that mean? Was he in trouble? Was he going to jail?

The kind police lady with the round face tried to hug him. 'It's okay, its okay,' she said, 'you will be fine. We'll find a nice family to look after you.'

She looked younger than he had first thought now she was close to him. He had thought all police officers were old and mean – that's what his mum had said.

Leo did not realise at this point, of course, that their paths would cross again in very different circumstances in the future.

As if Leo's mum knew what he was thinking, she suddenly became alive, not broken, not doubled in two, not as 'black and blue' as he had first thought.

Her voice was high, like it always was when she had taken some pills or drunk from the 'boozy' bottle.

'Say goodbye to him?' she screamed at the sergeant. 'Say goodbye … are you mad? Seven years I've spent trying to feed and clothe the little bastard, seven years of going without and putting up with beating after beating to try to tell myself I wanted him, wanted to be a normal mum, wanted to do the fuckin' school runs and play happy families. No! I DON'T want to say goodbye. I don't want to ever clap eyes on the little bastard again! Take him into protective custody, take him … do you hear me? Fuckin' take him and good riddance. He'll amount to no good. He was forced onto me by one of those no-hopers. I don't know why I ever kept him. I never wanted him in the first place, anyway.'

Leo was stunned. He had heard his mum call him names many times but never like this. This was hard, cold, and really mean.

As he watched the police officer lead her away, he thought he saw tears in her eyes. He told himself that she was sorry but deep down he knew that she had never loved him.

The words and contempt she had for him followed him, and they went on to haunt him for many years to come.

It was Halloween the night the round-faced police lady took him into protective custody, and he realised that it was his seventh birthday!

Happy birthday to the kid that nobody wanted. There had been no presents, no cake, and his mother hadn't even used his name, preferring to call him a 'little bastard'.

'I have a name, a lovely name, the one you gave to me,
A simple name, a charming name, for all the world to see.

And yet you never use my name, as if I weren't there,
The Kid, The Brat, The Bastard, I knew you did not care.

I have a name, a lovely name, well, that's what others say,
"That thing I bred, that nuisance", is what I hear each day.

I have a name, a lovely name, and in my dark despair
I use my name to soothe myself, 'cos no one else is there.

Why did you call me Leo? I think you got it wrong,
It stems from Latin origin, a lion brave and strong.

I have a name, a lovely name,
but I'm not brave and bold,
A child with no identity,
in a world that's hard and cold.'

CHAPTER 1

'THE GOOD' – THE FOSTER PARENTS

'No baby is born bad. All babies are beautiful, sweet, innocent, vulnerable, and solely reliant on adults to meet their needs and protect them.'

That had been Leo's start in life, hadn't it? Good! Of course, good!

Initially, after the night that 'The Knock' happened, when Leo was taken away, scared and unwanted, he had lived with a foster family.

The social workers were looking for a 'forever family' for him, an adoption!

There had been no fuss, no mother who fought to keep him. He was purely unwanted.

Leo hadn't minded his foster family, 'Ken and Angie'. There wasn't any screaming or groaning, no men coming and going. It was peaceful.

He did, however, wonder about the things he heard them say to his social workers.

He had been in the kitchen on one occasion. They had been in the adjoining room, and Leo heard Ken say,

'He seems angry. We have tried to talk to him, to tell him he's safe to express his emotions, but he just shakes his head. Sometimes he cries but then at other times he smiles, and we just hope that he is recovering.'

Leo knew what Ken meant. Sometimes he did cry. He would bury his head in Angie's lap and think about his mum. Why had she called him names? Why did she say she'd never wanted him?

Leo knew how she'd behaved was wrong, was unkind, bad, and he wasn't going to be bad like her or the men, so as he lived with Ken and Angie, over time he learned to say thank you for all the nice things they gave him, for the kind way in which they treated him.

He learned to be gentle with Ruby, the family dog, threw balls for her when out walking and helped to feed her each evening.

When he felt angry, as he sometimes did, he kept quiet. He did shake when he remembered those nights, his mum black and blue and the men who came and went, the screaming, the bruises, the 'obscenities', and he still picked his hands regularly.

Ken and Angie had fostered many children over many years. They had heard the worst things that there were to hear about what some unfortunate children went through at the hands of their parents.

They were trained in understanding how to deal with traumatised children and stress and attachment issues.

There was, however, something about Leo which troubled them. They had only looked after him for a short time when they realised there was a lot of healing to do, but nobody really listened to them. They were just the foster carers.

So, a short period of time passed. Leo was quiet in general and polite and well behaved, and the psychologists and the social workers felt that he was ready to move on to something more permanent, and a plan for adoption was made.

Ken and Angie wondered whether this was overly optimistic. In their experience, adoptions were usually pursued and were successful for younger children than Leo. Also, he had a complex and disturbing history, but who were they to argue? The professionals knew best, and it would be an amazing outcome for him if it worked.

When Angie tucked Leo into bed at night, she always felt the usual pang of pity and concern.

She had felt this emotion so many times over the years for so many abused and vulnerable children.

Leo tossed and turned in his sleep, so much that sometimes he cried and shouted. Sometimes his pillow was so wet that Angie had to replace it in the middle of the night.

Something occasionally troubled Ken and Angie even more, however, after a spell of crying and shouting, after one of them had comforted him, reassured him that he was safe, wiped away his tears.

Sometimes Leo's voice would change. Through the crying and moaning, his little-boy voice would disappear and a much deeper and more manly voice would emerge. It was so strange to hear, this little boy, now healthier looking after months of good care, with sweet cherub cheeks and a mass of dark curly hair. Sometimes he would articulate the voice of someone much older, someone aggressive and menacing. His language was really disturbing – 'Prostitute, whore, hooker, little bastard, fuckin' bitch, no-hoper, never wanted you anyway … unwanted, unwanted, unwanted,' and Leo would always be picking at his hands furiously as he chanted unconsciously.

Ken and Angie always documented these outbursts, these strange, disturbing outbursts which seemed to describe someone completely different to the vulnerable, kind and gentle little boy that they were looking after.

'He's bound to have night terrors, isn't he?' said the psychologists. 'He's been through so much; he just needs time.'

'He's always so kind and loving when conscious, isn't he?' argued the social workers. 'No sign of aggression when he's awake.'

Ken and Angie had to agree. Leo was a beautiful, loving, and vulnerable child, easy to look after, easy to take to heart.

And so it was, after a sad and unfortunate start to life, Leo was now to receive the childhood he deserved – adoptive parents, a forever mummy and daddy who would love him unconditionally and give him everything he needed and wanted.

So, despite their reservations, Ken and Angie were happy for Leo. A new start! A chance of a future a million miles from the poverty and abuse he had experienced.

They would miss him but hoped his new family would keep in touch. He was such a sweet boy.

Leo was scared as he left the warmth and security he had received from Ken and Angie over the last year, scared of what was to come and scared of the angry emotions which still stirred inside him.

'Goodbye ... goodbye.' Ken and Angie waved at Leo as the social worker led him away, away to his new life, his forever family, his mum and dad!

The 'Happy Ever After' ... so why did he feel so cold and alone? Where was his hope? Hope that things would turn out good!

Leo left foster care to start his new life on Halloween.
It was his eighth birthday!

> 'Hope confronts, it does not ignore pain,
> agony or injustice.
> You can't have hope without despair,
> because hope is a response.
> Hope is the active conviction that despair
> will never have the last word
> But despair can be cruel and persistent.'
> (Research)

CHAPTER 2

'WHEN GOOD IS MISUNDERSTOOD' – THE ADOPTIVE PARENTS

Eddie and Ingrid Twigg had been blessed when Lucy was born. Their beautiful baby girl, after years of trying to have a baby – Lucy had arrived.

Ingrid was thirty-nine at the time, after years of wanting a baby, tests, procedures, and IVF.

As time passed and they watched Lucy grow and develop, their parenting skills and confidence grew with her, and they started to wish for a second child, which they knew was impossible.

When Lucy was six, Eddie and Ingrid decided to explore the idea of adoption.

They spent a lot of time debating whether they could honestly love someone else's child as much as their own. They weren't sure, in fact they knew it was unlikely. They were honest with each other about that!

They wanted a sibling for Lucy. They were honest with each other about that also!

They wanted to ensure that Lucy had someone in later life when they were no longer around – honest again!

They were not quite as honest as they should have been, however, telling themselves they wanted another child for themselves when this was not the true and only reason.

They were very clear that Lucy was always to be their 'baby', so the adopted child needed to be an older child.

They knew from their research that adopters of older children were in demand; most people wanted babies.

They also knew that they had a lot to offer – a nice house, a successful family business, good parenting skills!

Yes, they were confident that this could work, but work for whom? For them? For Lucy? Or for some unfortunate child who needed a home?

They knew the answer, really, but did that make them bad?

Eddie and Ingrid flew through the adoption assessment process. They said all the right things, of course!

It took about nine months. It was intrusive, but they accepted being questioned and probed about every aspect of their lives, their circumstances, their finances, their motivation for wanting to adopt an older child.

Even their personal and most private details and thoughts were explored. They felt at times as though

they were 'baring their souls', and they did so carefully, very carefully indeed.

They wanted a child to love and cherish forever, another child to call their own, a child who would benefit in all ways from what they had to offer – love, security, and stability. Yes, they were well versed.

Lucy was spoken to as part of the process. This was the only time throughout the assessment when they worried a little. At nearly seven, Lucy could be headstrong. She was a 'demanding child' in the view of her school.

They preferred to call her 'bright and knowing her own mind'.

They didn't know what she would say when the social workers asked her about having a new brother or sister. They had really tried to sell the idea to her, how much fun it would be to have someone to play with and to look after her.

Lucy had objected to the idea from the outset, had stamped her feet and shouted angrily that she wasn't going to share her toys with any NEW brother or sister. Her friend, Darcy, had a brother, and Darcy's parents were always telling them to share things.

Oh *no*, Lucy was not keen on that idea at all.

Before the social workers arrived to talk to Lucy, Eddie and Ingrid had kept her calm, pacified her with sweets and a new doll – 'Plenty more where that came from.' They told her to be kind, to speak nicely to the social workers and say how nice it would be to share things. They told her to 'pretend' a little bit, like in her favourite book, *Teddy Pretends to go to the Fair.*

So, they basically told her to lie!

Then that was it, nine months in all, and then the adoption panel agreed – they were approved to adopt one child of either gender, age group six to ten years.

Plan accomplished, they were able to start considering the profiles of children waiting to be adopted.

Eddie and Ingrid had been told that this would be a time of great excitement for them, a time akin to being pregnant, waiting to meet your child – love, curiosity, planning, dreaming, and hoping all running through your veins.

Ingrid recalled her pregnancy with Lucy and could relate to these feelings, but this was not the same. This felt a bit more like an arrangement, a business transaction, even.

They were doing this for Lucy although Lucy did not know it.

Lucy did not make friends easily, and as Eddie and Ingrid were only children themselves, there was no one, really, once they got old, just a few cousins in Scotland, but they weren't close, barely a Christmas card sent.

No, it needed to be like this. An older brother or sister would be perfect. An adopted child would be grateful to them and would look on Lucy as a younger sibling, and they would of course make sure Lucy was looked after as a priority!

Eddie and Ingrid half-believed that what they were doing was good, was for some poor unfortunate child to have a loving home, but deep down they only really half-believed it themselves. They did not, of course, mention their hidden motive to the social workers, oh no! And when their marriage and the strength of their relationship was explored, Eddie's little 'indiscretions' all those years ago had been carefully hidden as well.

Oh, Ingrid had made Eddie pay again, of course. Just hearing someone ask, 'And how would you consider your relationship? What are your views on fidelity?' had been enough for Ingrid to go very cold once the social workers had gone home.

If only Eddie could have seen into the future and how the events of their lives were going to unfold through choosing to adopt a child, it would never have happened, of course!

But he did know from the start that their decision was flawed and not that good, really.

'Most people are good but occasionally they may do something that they know is bad.
(Research)

CHAPTER 3

'WHEN GOOD TURNS TO BAD' – A FOREVER FAMILY

When Eddie and Ingrid were sent Leo's profile, they were immediately interested.

'White British boy, aged seven, approaching eight. Following a negative and neglectful start in life, Leo is a kind, compassionate, and caring boy, who is seeking the love and stability of a forever home.'

They had viewed a few profiles of children needing adoptive parents. One described a boy aged nine, who was described as 'complex'. Oh, they knew what that meant – social-work jargon really meaning behavioral issues or trouble!

They had viewed the profiles of two girls. One was aged eight but 'needed a lot of time and attention to repair her from her previous trauma'. Well, Lucy would never buy into that.

A ten-year-old girl had caught their eye, but given her age, she had a strong sense of birth identity, and potential adopters were being asked to agree to contact with her natural parents once a year. No, that would never do. They would offer all the nice things in life and then she would probably return to live with her birth family when she was eighteen, oh no! That wasn't the idea at all.

So, Leo was looking very promising, and further exploration found that there would be no objection from his natural parents – **'Father unknown, mother doesn't want him, relinquished him without a fight.'**

So, Leo was unwanted – perfect!

When the introductions started, Leo was very shy. He clung to Ken and Angie.

At the first meeting, Eddie and Ingrid bought Leo a toy car and told him that they were his 'new mum and dad'. Leo hid his head in Angie's shoulder, trying not to look at them, trying to pretend it was not happening.

He already had a mum; where was she now? He hadn't seen her since that night, the night of the grunting and screaming, the night the police came, and she was black and blue and said she'd never wanted him in the first place.

The social worker had tried to arrange contact visits in the early days, after Leo first went to live with Ken and Angie, but he realised very quickly that his mum had meant what she said. She did not want him; she had never wanted him!

The pain in his chest at this realisation was too much to bear, and now here he was, being introduced to a new mum and dad. He'd never had a dad – what would that be like?Ken, his foster carer, was kind and what Leo imagined he would want a father to be, but it seemed as though Ken and Angie didn't want him either. Why couldn't they keep him?

Leo was struggling to understand why nobody wanted him. Why was he so unwanted?

Leo moved to live with his forever family on his eighth birthday, after two weeks of coming and going to their house to supposedly get to know them.

The social worker drove him there in what felt like a cold and clinical manner, just her last job of the day.

It was Halloween.

Leo had received therapy while he had lived with Ken and Angie. He knew that his early life had been neglectful – that was the word the therapist had used. It seemed a simple word, really, just a single word which described how it felt to be on your own, in the dark, often cold, sometimes hungry, while the men came and went.

The grunting, the shouting, the bruises, the obscenities, bastard, unwanted ... all being described in one word – 'neglectful'. It didn't seem enough, really!

As he had waved goodbye to Ken and Angie, that familiar feeling in the pit of his stomach hit him again and he started to pick at his hands furiously.

It shouldn't have been worse than the night the police came, should it?

He wasn't hungry, or scared, or cold. No-one had been hurt, there was no grunting or screaming, but somehow he felt a sense of foreboding without even knowing what that meant.

The therapist could call it neglectful if that's what he thought, but Leo knew what it was. It was ... unwanted, unwanted, unwanted.

Eddie and Ingrid made a fuss of Leo initially as he arrived. 'Two celebrations in one go,' they said.

'Your birthday and your new forever family – us.'

There had been balloons and a cake. It should have felt like a warm feeling, a feeling of belonging, a feeling of being 'wanted', but something wasn't right. Eddie and Ingrid kept looking at Lucy nervously, and she, Lucy, just looked straight through Leo as if he weren't there.

After they had all eaten cake, Ingrid asked Leo if he would like to help her put things away in his room – his things, his clothes, toys and belongings which Angie had bought him.

Ingrid said he could arrange his room however he wanted, choose a new duvet cover, and they would decorate the room however he chose.

Leo felt that maybe this could have been done before he arrived. They knew what he liked; he had heard Ken and Angie telling them.

Leo suddenly felt tired, really, really tired. He was only eight years old and healthy, so the adoption medical had said, but he didn't feel eight and healthy. He felt much, much older and quite weary.

When Leo told Ingrid he didn't want to help sort out his room, that he was tired and just wanted to go to bed, he thought he saw a funny look come over her face. He couldn't describe it. Was she unhappy because he was tired!

He thought about his mum, his real mum. She liked him to be tired, liked him to go to his little room under the stairs and be quiet and go to sleep. He could not understand mothers at all!

Ingrid was looking at Eddie now, a look which said, 'Well, do something; talk to him.'

Lucy was looking from her mum to her dad with a satisfied look on her face. She saw trouble afoot.

'Well, Ingrid,' said Eddie, 'I bet the lad is tired. It's been a big day.' Eddie smiled at Leo, a kind smile, a nod. 'Why don't we leave sorting out your room until tomorrow?'

Leo felt grateful. He forced a weak smile and nodded at Eddie, but Ingrid wasn't happy. Leo just knew she wasn't happy, but nonetheless he had the overwhelming desire to lie down there and then and go to sleep for a very long time.

Leo barely remembered much more of that first night. He knew it was Eddie who took him up to bed, said 'Goodnight,' in a matter-of-fact manner and just left him there like he was someone much older than eight.

There was no tucking in, no cuddles or bedtime story like Angie used to do. Leo might as well be back in the cupboard, really.

As Leo dozed off, he knew it was still early. It was dark outside, but he could still hear the laughter of Halloween activities going on outside.

Someone knocked on the door a few times, and Leo heard childish voices say, 'Trick or treat!' He heard Lucy giggling and Ingrid chastising the children who had knocked on the door too loudly.

Leo heard children out on the street shouting, 'House of the dead, house of the dead!' and thought that it must be some sort of Halloween game. He realised he was picking his hands furiously again.

As tiredness engulfed him, Leo didn't know how he felt – shattered emotions, an inability to trust, anticipation, fear, but he didn't understand any of these emotions, of course. He only knew he was more tired than he could ever remember in his life, and despite the forever family who had 'chosen' him, he still felt unwanted!

Downstairs, Ingrid and Eddie were looking at each other, looks which an outsider might wonder about.

The looks implied that they didn't know what the other one was thinking. They were looks of uncertainty, each searching the other's expression to try to get an understanding.

Lucy was in the bath, splashing around among pink bubbles and bath toys.

'Ten minutes,' Ingrid said, 'then it's time for pyjamas and a story.'

The scene downstairs looked like the perfect family evening except for the sad little boy lying alone upstairs.

'He's bound to be exhausted, for God's sake,' said Eddie to his wife, but almost under his breath, almost a mumble.

Ingrid was louder; no mumbling from her. 'Well, I'm telling you now, Ed,' she said, 'I only asked him to help with his room. I mean, it is *his* room. He should have been bloody grateful.'

Eddie sighed. Ingrid had wanted to adopt so badly it was like once she had set her mind to it, that was it, no objections accepted.

Eddie liked the idea, he did. The boy needed a good home, and although he could never voice this to Ingrid, it wouldn't do Lucy any harm at all to learn to share, to be kind, and to realise that other people mattered too.

Lucy was the centre of their world. Without a doubt she was. It was as though she were a miracle, plucked from heaven at the right time, a time in their lives when Eddie had thought Ingrid might never get over his little indiscretions!

Eddie's mind was wandering now, back to the days when the only time Ingrid allowed him near her was to try for a baby. It was a soul-destroying time. She was a woman on a mission and there was no love, affection, or sensuality about it.

He was the male, the sire, expected to be able to produce!

God, she was hard in those days, hard as nails. The looks of sheer disappointment and resentment when each month the tests were negative, NOT pregnant, no baby on the way.

At least once Lucy eventually arrived, she was softer, less hard, not so bitter, and this made things bearable.

Without Lucy, Ingrid would never have forgiven him. Looking back, Eddie couldn't understand why he had used prostitutes. It wasn't like they offered any love or affection, and it was not like he'd done it that much. It was the opposite of the love and affection he was seeking, it was sordid, a quick fumble, as quick as the sex worker could make it! And God, the conditions of those houses, the stink, the poverty. He should be ashamed, but he had paid them, lessened their plight, that's what he had told himself, that's how he had eased his conscience, and at least he had some sort of control, got to choose when he wanted sex, and what sort of sex. Ingrid had never been particularly adventurous in that area!

Bringing himself back to the present, Eddie felt Ingrid looking at him. He had been deep in thought, and she probably thought he was thinking about the boy, ahh yes, the boy!

The adoption had progressed quite quickly, faster than either of them had expected. It was like the bloody social workers couldn't get it over and done with quickly enough!

They probably got praised at work, maybe got a bonus – conspiracists would say this.

'Loving couple save unwanted unloved child.'

'Bloody heroes, aren't they, the social workers,' Eddie thought cynically.

No-one had spoken to the boy about the family business though. Not everyone's cup of tea, is it, running an undertakers.

The boy would get used to it; another way he would be useful as he grew up. There was no one else to take over the family business, was there? Lucy was never going to embalm dead bodies and polish coffins, was she? Not bloody likely!

Eddie had shooed the kids off earlier, the local lot, standing outside chanting, 'House of the dead.'

He wished they wouldn't call it that. He didn't know if the boy had heard from his bedroom – hopefully not. He was bound to be exhausted and fast asleep.

Yes, Eddie thought, he had done the right thing ushering Leo off to bed. There was time to celebrate his birthday properly another day.

His thoughts started to drift again. The boy's misfortune was certainly plain to see – unloved, unwanted, born on Halloween, sullen and moody but potentially willing to do as they wanted!

Eddie smiled over at Ingrid, a satisfied smile. They had achieved what they had set out to do – a sibling for Lucy and now maybe even someone to follow in his footsteps as an undertaker. The business had been in Eddie's family for years, and he hoped it would be so for years to come.

Ingrid, however, had that strange look on her face. Eddie couldn't fathom it. When they were younger, he used to find it intriguing, wondering what the strange look meant – half-smile, half-frown, almost a grimace.

It wasn't an expression which Eddie saw regularly, only at certain times in Ingrid's life, times when she was satisfied with something, and if he were honest, it was usually times when she had power and control.

If he were really honest, there was a way to describe Ingrid's expression, but he didn't want to. Thoughts of the past came back, such as when his parents had been ill, and Ingrid thought that they had been 'demanding', when actually they were dying.

Thoughts also came back of when the neighbour's cat had left its excrement in their garden, and Ingrid had viciously flung the cat over the fence as it scratched and hissed at her.

The cat had to be put down from its injuries after being flung.

If he were exceptionally honest, Eddie knew what the look on Ingrid's face portrayed. It was cruelty.

Ingrid's expression gave him a niggle, because he wondered if she was going to direct her vengeance on the boy, and he didn't want to start having misgivings about the adoption at this early stage. It was only the first day.

But Eddie was troubled by the look on her face because of the past!

'Inside each of us there is a seed of both good and evil. It is a constant struggle as to which one will win. One cannot exist without the other.' (Research)

CHAPTER 4

'WHEN BAD GETS WORSE' – UNWANTED AGAIN

Leo woke and wasn't quite sure where he was at first.

The daylight was visible through his thin curtains, but he had slept well.

There had been no screaming, no beatings, in fact, it was just as calm as at Ken and Angie's house.

Leo didn't realise he had probably been exhausted, and he wasn't sure whether he had heard or dreamt children chanting, 'House of the dead, house of the dead!' the night before.

As he looked around his new bare bedroom with none of his belongings in it yet, he supposed it wasn't so bad, but the ache in his chest left him feeling as though something were missing. He couldn't describe it. Leo didn't recognise it as the empty feeling of not having a loving mother or father.

He had never had a 'primary attachment figure' – that's what he had heard the social workers say.

'Attachment difficulties; attachment disorder.' That was their jargon.

He recalled the night the police came and took him. He remembered the big, bulky police officer saying,

'Poor little sod. Doesn't look like anyone has ever loved him or cared for him.'

Leo didn't know that these two responses went hand in hand, because being unwanted led to attachment difficulties.

'Poor attachment is just another name for disappointment and pain.' (Research)

Leo just knew that something was missing. He had heard someone say once, 'You never miss what you have never had,' but he didn't think that was true. He couldn't verbalise it and he couldn't understand it, but he knew that it made him sad and very, very angry.

He'd never had a mother's love. He had rarely ever been kissed or cuddled. He had never been made to feel special, 'loved unconditionally' – that's what they called it, wasn't it?

No, he'd never had that, but the empty feeling in the pit of his stomach, the gut-wrenching feeling inside told him that he had missed out on something which every child deserves.

It was there, it was real, and it ate away at him over and over again as he lay alone, picking at his hands furiously.

When he had been at Ken and Angie's, when he was a foster child, the feeling had eased a bit. The feeling eased when Angie took him up to bed at night. It eased when she kissed his cheek and said, 'Goodnight, lovey.'

So here he was, his first morning in his new forever home, lying alone, and he did not know what to expect.

Leo looked out of the window, and although it was a sunny day for the first day of November, there was a chill in the air, a chill you might expect for this time of year, but there was something else as well, and he could not put his finger on it.

Leo didn't know what he was supposed to do now. No-one had told him what he was supposed to do.

Should he stay in his bedroom until someone called him? Should he call someone? Should he go downstairs?

He suddenly felt really angry again. No-one had told him what he was supposed to bloody do.

It seemed like forever that Leo sat on his bed in his new home, nothing much around him, just thinking about what he should do and picking at his hands.

Suddenly, after what felt like an eternity, Leo heard Eddie's voice calling him. 'Are you up, lad? Are you okay? Come on now, come downstairs for your breakfast.'

Leo found himself leaping up off the bed. He could easily have bounded out of the room. He wanted to be out of here, he wanted his breakfast, he wanted to know what his new life looked like, but he steadied himself and tried not to run. He had an instinctive feeling that Ingrid would not approve of an eight-year-old boy charging through her house, even if he was supposed to be *her* eight-year-old boy, *her* new son, the child that *she* wanted to love and cherish and adopt. No, despite all of this, he did not think that Ingrid would approve, and so he went slowly and approached the stairs and then the kitchen with caution.

When he opened the door to the kitchen, they were all there, his new MOTHER, his new FATHER, and his new SISTER. They were all sitting around the small kitchen dining table. The table had four chairs around it, but it looked as though it were really only big enough for three. The fourth chair was smaller and had been squeezed in.

Lucy sat in the chair furthest away from the empty chair, the smallest chair, the squeezed-in chair, the one brought in from the garage as an afterthought, the one meant for him!

Eddie beckoned Leo to sit down, and he did as he was bid.

Ingrid was smiling, a strange smile which didn't quite reach her eyes. 'Did you sleep well, Leo?' she asked half-politely, half-curtly.

Leo nodded. He muttered, 'Yes,' under his breath. It was barely more than a whisper.

Lucy just looked at him. She said nothing. It was as though he weren't there as she said to her mother, 'Can I have some more toast, please?' and Ingrid immediately jumped up from her own chair to make it for her.

Eddie passed Leo a bowl of cereal and half-muttered to Ingrid, 'Make the lad some toast as well, love.'

The words weren't warm, but they weren't cold, just a mutter, a request, nothing out of the ordinary.

Both Eddie and Ingrid, however, stared lovingly at Lucy, who remained ambivalent toward Leo, no eye contact, no smile, no signals of warmth at all – a cold little girl!

Leo's mind started to wander as he ate his toast. He wondered what it would be like to be born into a family where you had a mum and dad of your own and where both could look lovingly at you, as if you were the most precious thing in the world, sheer, bare, raw, and obvious love, even around the breakfast table, the bloody breakfast table, which only seemed big enough for three people, not four.

Leo felt the knot in the pit of his stomach start to tighten. The anger was starting to consume him again.

If Lucy had been less cold and unwelcoming, if Ingrid had made him some toast without being asked, if his chair had been the same size as the other three, would things have turned out differently!

Leo tried to eat his toast, but he couldn't swallow. The knot was tightening because he knew that his stomach wouldn't accept the food he was trying to eat, despite being hungry.

He placed the toast back onto his plate. He used a spoon to mix the cereals round and round, mixing them together with the milk until they looked like a soggy mess.

He could feel that Eddie and Ingrid were looking at him although his head was bowed low, looking into the cereal bowl and plate of toast.

'Not hungry, lad? Don't you want to eat something?' Eddie's voice sounded nervous. What could Eddie be nervous about? Eddie, the man whose life was so perfect that he could adopt a child, an unwanted child.

Leo wanted to start laughing now. His thoughts took him back to the night the police came and took him, the night it all ended, or started, depending on which way one looked at it. It was a year ago now, a year since he had *really* found out that his mother had never wanted him … never fuckin' loved him … unwanted, unwanted, unwanted.

Leo directed his stare at Lucy now, not Ingrid, not Eddie, no, straight at Lucy as he said, 'No, thanks, I am not hungry. I am not fuckin' hungry at all.'

Even Leo didn't recognise his own voice, the angry, aggressive voice, which sounded like a man and not a child!

He stifled the urge to giggle. Lucy's face was a picture. Eddie's face was a picture! But it was Ingrid who spoke, and when she spoke it was with cold, hard precision. 'Don't you dare blaspheme in this house, boy. Don't you ever dare again, do you hear me?'

Don't these idiots know I have a name, thought Leo but said nothing, as Ingrid looked like she might explode.

Lucy was looking at her mother with a curious expression on her face, as if she were wondering what was coming next.

Eddie was looking at his wife with trepidation, clearly anxious about what might be coming next.

Nonetheless, Leo still had the overwhelming desire to laugh, even though he was picking at his hands furiously.

The silence seemed to go on for an eternity until Ingrid spoke again. 'Did you hear me, boy? Did you hear what I said?' Her voice was not now as precise, more high-pitched and hysterical.

Leo wondered whether this was because he had 'blasphemed' or whether it was because he had used the tone he had used, or was it simply because she wasn't used to anyone ignoring her? Maybe it was all three.

'WELL?' The sheer bellow of Ingrid's tone now made Leo, Eddie, and even Lucy jump!

Leo knew he had to answer, so who should he be – the sweet little boy or the aggressive man? He wasn't consciously making a choice. His reactions, his responses, were not understood by him.

Leo didn't know who he was, and he didn't know who he wanted to be. There were so many things that he couldn't make sense of.

Sometimes he talked to himself in the mirror. He had started doing this when he was very young, when he was on his own for long periods of time. It was like company, really. He would ask himself a question and then give himself an answer. He never knew what voice he would use, because he wasn't in control of it.

Leo smiled to himself cynically at the thought. No wonder he didn't belong anywhere; no wonder no-one fuckin' wanted him.

Ingrid noticed the wry little smile. She saw it immediately as insolence, but she did not address it this time. She turned to Lucy and calmly told her to leave the kitchen and go to her room.

Lucy didn't want to, although she had been shocked at the boy's outburst. She was excited. She wanted to know what would happen next. Her mother had never used the tone she had just used to her, but she knew at nearly seven years old only that her mother could be hard and spiteful, oh yes, she had learned that when she had listened to her parents arguing.

Lucy didn't understand the arguments. She didn't know what a 'whore' was, but young though she was, she knew her mother could be cruel with words.

Her mother's voice was still calm when she asked Lucy to leave the kitchen for the second time, and Lucy knew she needed to do as she had been asked.

Once Lucy had left, Ingrid turned to Eddie, not so calm now, much less in control as she boomed, 'Ed, what do you propose to do about the way the boy has just behaved?'

Eddie knew the onus was on him. He was still shocked by what Leo had said and how he had said it, in that strange, aggressive, adult voice. He knew, however, that he was supposed to do something about it, but he didn't know what!

His empathic side suddenly swamped him. The poor kid, unwanted, unloved, he was bound to have heard bad language, the way he had been reared.

42

Eddie looked over to where Leo was still sitting at the table. He couldn't work out the expression on Leo's face – was it fear? Was it nervousness? He just couldn't tell, but he knew that Ingrid would be expecting him to come down hard on the boy. Oh yes, 'Start as you mean to go on,' would be Ingrid's motto.

'We're giving him a home, saving him from himself and the life he would have had in the gutter.' Yes, Ingrid had been very clear, behind closed doors of course, well away from the social workers.

Just as Eddie was about to address Leo, to ask him to apologise for swearing, to ask him not to do it again, suddenly Leo spoke first, in a quiet voice, a little boy's voice, meek, as he said again, 'No, I'm not hungry, thank you, and I'm sorry I used expletives.' He said the word slowly and with meaning, but his voice remained young and innocent.

'Oh, well now,' said Eddie, somewhat relieved despite being surprised, 'as long as you're sorry and you don't do it again, let's leave it at that. We know you must be finding everything new and strange.'

Leo didn't realise that he was wearing a very satisfied look on his face. He had never really understood how to regulate his emotions – how could he have?

But something was dawning on him. It was a slow realisation, very slow, almost like waiting for an answer which you know you are probably not going to get.

Leo realized that during the last twenty minutes, the last bloody painful unwanted twenty minutes, he had developed some power. He didn't realise or recognise it as power, as he had never experienced power in the whole of his young life so far, but as he looked at Ingrid's face, an angry face,

43

contorted almost like a caricature, he realised that what he said and how he said it made an impact on others.

This truly was enlightening and empowering for him. Leo, the unwanted little bastard, could evoke feelings, responses, and emotions in others.

As he looked from Ingrid to Eddie, Ingrid's face angry and Eddie's face pleading for all of this to be over, Leo felt a warm feeling, a new feeling, a feeling of control.

Ingrid bellowed, 'Well, is that IT, Ed? Is that all you've got to say? The boy has sworn, he has been rude and arrogant, which I suppose he can't help due to being dragged up, but really, Ed, IS THAT IT?'

Eddie signalled to Leo to leave the kitchen and go upstairs, and it dawned on Leo that for all his young life so far, he had always done as he was told. When his real mother had told him to shut up and be quiet because she had a man in, he just did it.

When the men who came and went saw him briefly and told him to stop snivelling – 'Snotty-nosed little brat' – he just did it.

When the police officers who took him away that night told him, 'Come along with us now, son, it will be okay,' he just did it.

Even when Ken and Angie made requests of him, although they were reasonable requests – 'Come on, Leo, let's brush our teeth, let's get ready for school' – it never dawned on him that he could actually say no to anyone or anything. Never did that dawn on him, so he just did it!

Sitting in the kitchen now with his new mother and father, Leo suddenly felt differently to how he had ever felt before.

Here was a woman so angry that he thought she would burst and a man who was so weak that he just wanted everything to be as peaceful as it could be, no matter the cost.

Yet Leo wasn't scared, he wasn't picking his hands, not at all. He felt an almighty strength, a feeling which was so new to him that it almost made him lightheaded.

'Leo,' said Eddie, 'run along now, there's a good boy. Go off to your room while mum and I talk about things.'

Eddie was determined to try to defuse the situation, for the sake of everyone. He was starting to feel very uncomfortable with the boy's demeanor all of a sudden, and Ingrid, well, he knew that look. He knew she had been pushed to her limit by the boy's disconcerting attitude toward her! He had seen that look before, oh, indeed he had. He pictured in his mind the neighbour's limp and lifeless cat.

Eddie had no idea what Ingrid might do. If she laid a hand on the boy out of sheer temper, things could go badly wrong. He wasn't their legal child yet.

'Please, Leo,' Eddie was even more pleading than he knew, 'there's a good boy.'

Leo decided that he would do as he was asked, not because he wanted to and not because he needed to. A strange new feeling had come over him today, and he knew he was going to use it to his advantage, my God, yes, he was!

However, for today, he was going to do as he was asked, because this was going to be a fun game!

This was going to be about him seeking some sort of revenge for the life he had endured so far, but he would do it slowly at his own pace.

Leo didn't realise that the storm raging within him was likely to lead to no good, no good at all.

'Okay, DAD.' He emphasised the word 'Dad' before shooting a knowing look at his new mother and then leaving the kitchen slowly and precisely at his own pace.

Eddie didn't dare look at Ingrid. He felt as though he were in a minefield, not knowing when or exactly how the explosion might happen or what harm it might do when it exploded.

He needed to think, he needed to think quickly on his feet, think fast.

He tried to sound lighthearted as he said, 'Crikey, Ing, I didn't see that coming. It must all be too much for him. The social workers never said anything about angry outbursts, did they?'

Ingrid inhaled slowly, as if she were taking the biggest breath she could before she said through gritted teeth, 'No, they didn't, did they? Not a word!'

'Everyone has two sides, good and evil. How you treat me will determine which side you get to see.' (Research)

CHAPTER 5

'WHEN BAD GETS UGLY' –
THE REALISATION

Leo had been living with his adoptive family for around eleven months before the final adoption order was granted. This was apparently longer than usual!

He had heard conversations between his 'mum' and 'dad' and the endless different social workers who came and went from time to time.

The realisation hit him somewhere around the third month of being there. Although uncomfortable from the start, Leo had still made himself believe that his new 'forever' family really wanted him. He had needed to believe this, despite 'Mum' appearing more and more detached as time went by, Lucy's indifference toward him and 'Dad's' indifference. They had chosen him, hadn't they!

They had wanted a little boy to love, and he was that little boy. He willed himself to believe this. He told himself every night as he lay lonely in his room, *THEY LOVE ME. THEY WANTED ME.*

However, the picking of his hands came back with a vengeance, and the waiting for the feeling of belonging never came, despite what he told himself.

The new feeling of power, which he had felt surge through him on that very first day, lay festering.

When the social workers visited, 'Mum' and 'Dad' said all the right things, how much they loved him, how he made their lives complete, blah, blah, blah.

Leo felt sure that he had been there about three months when he had learned the real truth, the sad, devastating realisation that they didn't love him or really want him at all!

It was a cold, dark night in January. It reminded him of Halloween, with the darkness setting in before he even got home from school.

Home was always a bit depressing although Leo didn't understand the concept, just a simple tea, usually alone, then instructions to do his homework and then bed, not much of an existence really but at least he was safe.

Lucy, of course, did after-school activities such as gymnastics, dance, and athletics. It had started to amaze Leo that the social workers who came and went never sat and talked to him, never asked him what life was like, not that he would have told them anyway. He hadn't got anyone else who wanted or loved him, and at least the horrible dirty men didn't come and go.

Once he had settled into his new life, however, he found himself thinking more and more about his real mum, his mum who had never wanted him.

That last night, how she had called him names, obscenities, the look in her eyes, and yet he was sure she had been crying.

Leo didn't really understand his feelings of anger. He knew something was bubbling inside of him, but he could not have known that it would end so badly!

Leo did not know what he was capable of when his emotions took over, although he gained some insight into this on that night, the night that the realisation set in!

On that night, he learned that he had the ability to destroy, to *really* destroy and hurt!

That night was the turning point, although he didn't recognise it, only three months into his new 'adoptive and forever' home, where he had been told that he was to be loved and cherished unconditionally until adulthood ... and beyond.

It was as he had heard them talking that night that something really changed. It was the night that real anger consumed him, took over his very being and never really left again.

The feeling was like a great big tidal wave, washing over him, drowning him, leaving him unable to breathe or get free, despite thrashing, kicking, and trying to scream. He was trapped with feelings of pure anguish and terror.

Leo had thought his behaviour on that first day, when he had sworn and refused to go to his room, was the worst he could ever behave, but he had been wrong ... very, very wrong!

The evening had started like any other one: home from school, tea at the table – plenty of room now, as there was only him sitting around it, as Lucy was at a sports event.

Leo couldn't get interested in sport. Even if anyone had bothered to encourage him, no way could he undress in front of others. He just couldn't.

The first time he had been asked to get changed for P.E. at his new school he just froze; he was horrified!

The P.E. teacher had been kind, had reassured him it was fine and had let him get dressed and undressed in private. 'It's okay, lad, don't worry,' said the teacher. He must have known, that kind teacher, he must have known Leo's shame.

That kind teacher must have known that somehow, getting dressed and undressed related to Leo's past, made him think of all those nights when he had lived with his 'real' mother, when the men had come and gone, the grunts, the screaming, the bruises … black and blue!

So, there was no way he was getting dressed and undressed in front of other people. The kind teacher had made exceptions for P.E., but there was no way Leo was getting involved in sporting activities. He didn't need to anyway – no-one asked or encouraged him, and from that night, the realisation night, three months after arriving at his FOREVER HOME, his bloody fuckin' god-forsaken FOREVER HOME … he knew nobody cared!

After Leo had eaten his tea alone – sandwiches with a cheap meat spread on them and an orange – he sat at the table for a while, knowing that when 'Mum' came in from the lounge or when 'Dad' arrived back with Lucy, it would be, 'Come on now, haven't you got homework to do?' and so he sat for a while, letting his mind drift back to his mother, his *real* mother, his fuckin' mother who had given birth to him but never wanted him.

Where was she now? Was she alive? Had one of the men killed her? Did she regret things? Did she miss him? They were the same old thoughts as Leo realised he was picking at his hands again.

Leo looked around the kitchen. He had been here for about three months now, and every evening after school he sat at this table, but he felt as though he had never really looked around before.

He had known from the first night that this table was too small for four people. He remembered thinking that the first night he arrived, it was just as if he had been squashed in as an afterthought on a mismatched chair.

Leo thought it was hilarious, looking back. *Why didn't they just get a bigger fuckin' table if they wanted me so much?* He felt a cynical smile spread over his face. Of course they didn't get a bigger table; they didn't need a bigger table, because other than that first night, or when the social workers visited, they never all sat around it together anyway!

Leo's eyes wandered now to a cupboard next to the back door. Well, he assumed it was a cupboard – it looked like one. On this evening, something struck him about the cupboard door. It reminded him of his bedroom, the one from his old home with his real mum, where the men had come and gone.

Before that final night, when Leo was taken, he remembered someone saying, 'Where the kid sleeps, it's hardly a bedroom, is it? More like a cupboard.' He thought it was a social worker who said it, or a police officer. He couldn't really remember or differentiate.

Without really thinking, Leo rose from the table and walked over to the kitchen cupboard. He'd never looked inside before, never bothered. He had heard other kids at school talk about taking crisps or biscuits from their cupboards at home, either with or without their parents' consent, but the thought had never occurred to him. He had enough to eat. He didn't ever feel hungry like he used to, he had breakfast, school dinner and a sandwich for tea, more than enough, more than he had ever had.

So, as he approached the cupboard, it was not with any intention of looking for food or treats, but suddenly without any reasoning why, Leo felt compelled to look inside.

As he placed his hand on the door handle, trepidation coursed through him, although he didn't recognise it as such and wouldn't have understood why even if he did.

When he tried to open the door, it didn't open at first, and he thought it was locked. He pulled on it harder, however, and realised it was just sticking a bit. As he pulled on it forcefully it opened readily, and he looked inside.

Leo didn't know what he had been expecting to find in the cupboard. He had by now got used to the fact that Eddie was an undertaker and that the adjoining property to the kitchen was where dead bodies were kept. He had got used to the local kids chanting, 'House of the dead, house of the dead!'

Leo wasn't bothered about dead bodies essentially being in the next room. It caused him no concern or fear. He didn't care about dead people. He wanted living people to be nicer, to be kinder, to love him, to want him!

As he peered into the cupboard, however, he suddenly felt anxious. It was dark. He couldn't see a light switch, so he couldn't really see what was inside. Leo smiled to himself at the thought that 'Dad' might have put some dead bodies in there, and he almost laughed out loud when his searching hand found the light switch and the cupboard suddenly lit up!

Tins of tomatoes and beans were stacked on a shelf on one side and cleaning products were neatly set out on a shelf on the opposite side. The back wall was bare and the whole cupboard was about the same size as his old bedroom had been. No dead bodies in sight. Leo sniggered to himself.

Suddenly, however, Leo had the desire to lie down. He didn't know where this desire came from, but it was there, and it was overwhelming! Why the hell did he want to lie down in this stupid bloody little cupboard? But he did, and he also wanted a blanket to pull over him. He wanted to feel like he used to feel, but he couldn't understand it; there was no logic at all. Why would he want to feel like he used to feel when he was scared and hungry, listening to the men come and go, the grunting the screaming, the bruises ... black and blue?

Why would he want to remember the names his mother had called him the night the police came, when she said she had never wanted him in the first place. 'I don't ever want to clap eyes on the little bastard again.'

It made no sense. Why would he want to remember those terrible days, that terrible night? And yet, consciously or subconsciously, Leo slowly lay down on the floor of the cupboard. His head had started feeling funny, and the anger, which he didn't recognise as such, was ever present!

Once lying down and curled into the foetal position, Leo started talking to himself. He started to mutter, 'Prostitute, hooker, whore,' and as he lay there, the anger which engulfed him made him feel weak and faint ... unwanted, unwanted, unwanted!

Leo didn't know how long he laid there. He wanted a blanket, but there was no blanket. *That was funny*, he thought to himself as he picked at his hands, *why would he want a blanket, a thin dirty blanket like he used to have. Why would he want one of those!*

Suddenly, with all these thoughts, emotions, and anger flooding through him, Leo was brought back to reality when he heard voices entering the kitchen. It was 'Mum' and 'Dad', his *fuckin' forever* parents, and he was startled as he was brought back into the reality of the situation.

As Leo lay there wondering what to do, he realised the light was off. He didn't remember switching the light off. He must have done so without realising. He was used to the dark, afterall!

The voices became louder, and they were getting clearer, no mistaking 'Mum's' dulcet tones and 'Dad's' quieter voice, resigned and usually always ready to agree with his wife.

'What are we going to do then, Ed?' said Ingrid. 'It's been three months. You know what they're like, the bloody social workers. They will start asking.'

'What about?' said Eddie questioningly. 'You mean about the adoption order?'

'Yes, of course about the bloody adoption order,' said Ingrid, irritated. 'We have said everything is going well, and the twelve weeks have passed, so the expectation is that we will finalise the adoption with the final order.'

Leo lay perfectly still, dead still, remaining in exactly the same position on the floor of the cupboard, not moving a muscle, hardly daring to breathe.

He knew a little bit about the adoption order – one of the social workers had explained to him. 'Life Story work' they had called it. It should have been called 'Shit Story' in his case, he remembered thinking!

She was okay, actually, the social worker who had explained things to him. She was quite young, with kind eyes. Leo remembered thinking that she probably hadn't been doing the job for very long, still being enthusiastic and wanting to help.

'You see, Leo,' she had said, 'we must be absolutely sure that the decisions we make for you are the right ones, be certain that this is the right forever home for you. That is why you live here for a few months before any final adoption order is made.'

Oh yes, Leo had thought, *I am on trial … fuckin' trial –* '*Try Before You Buy*'!

Leo knew for sure that it wasn't a case of whether the decision was right for him. It was much more likely that it was whether it was right for Ingrid and Eddie, oh, and Lucy, let's not forget *darling* Lucy.

The voices of 'Mum and Dad' were getting even closer now, and Leo thought they must be almost right outside the cupboard door. He resisted the urge to giggle but didn't help himself when he pictured in his mind what would happen if he suddenly flew out of the cupboard and startled them, ran at them, fists pounding, screaming at them, hitting them, lashing out to *hurt* them!

Leo wasn't sure whether he was actually forming a plan or just fantasising, but just as he was thinking about what to do next, just as he was getting cold and uncomfortable on the cupboard floor, 'Mum' and 'Dad' carried on talking.

Leo smothered the idea of laughing out loud again. It was as if he weren't there! AS IF HE WEREN'T THERE. So hilarious. They had no bloody idea that he was there!

As Leo heard 'Mum' speak again, her voice nearer, getting louder, his thoughts of jumping out subsided, and he became the vulnerable little boy he had always been as he heard her words.

Voice booming, hard, cold, it was the vicious tone of his mother, *his mother*, the second one he had had, and he was only eight.

This 'mum' seemed almost colder and more uncaring than the original one. Leo stifled the urge to giggle again. The 'original one' – how many kids had an 'original mother', one who called them names and gave them away gratefully to the police?

Leo's emotions were overtaking him now – hysteria, sadness, anger … oh yes … ANGER!

He took a sharp breath as he heard 'Mum' boom, 'THE EXPECTATIONS, THE BLOODY ADOPTION ORDER! Well, we might have had our own agenda for taking the kid. Maybe we weren't completely honest about wanting someone to look after Lucy when we got old. Maybe we didn't tell them about your little INDISCRETIONS … but what about them then, ED? The bloody social workers – what about them? WHAT THEY DIDN'T TELL US!'

'Mum's' voice sounded vicious. Leo could tell that both of them were very close to the cupboard now, very close to possibly opening the door and finding him there, listening to them.

Oh yes, he was listening to them all right, and somewhere deep inside of him, somewhere in the dark, dark place of his inner emotions, a realisation was dawning on him!

'Mum' continued now, and Leo wasn't sure whether her anger was directed at 'Dad' or him or actually at the social workers who had clearly palmed him off on them.

'Mum' continued, 'They didn't bother telling us, did they, that the kid was sullen and unloving, nothing to give, no gratitude, no thank you for taking him on when nobody else bloody wanted him? I'm telling you, Ed, if we're taking him on, if we are going through with their BLOODY ADOPTION ORDER, then the kid needs to start being more grateful and start doing more around here. We are not a charity.'

That was it. That was it. The realisation now hit Leo like a bullet. Suddenly, he understood his emotions as if he were someone much older than he was.

He realised exactly what was going on. He struggled not to scream, struggled not to bolt out of the cupboard and run. God, he wanted to run, run, run, run anywhere out of here, but he had nowhere to go, of course. Unwanted, unwanted, unwanted!

The social worker was a liar, 'Mum and Dad' were liars, everyone he knew was a liar. They didn't want him at all. They certainly didn't love him 'like he was their own'!

What a joke. What a fuckin' joke. 'Love him like he was their own.' That's what the social workers had said!

As Leo gasped at the realisation, his body started fidgeting and he no longer cared whether he was quiet or not. He no longer cared if they found him lying on the floor in the cupboard. They could do what they liked, oh yes, they could! There was no way he was staying here. No way was he carrying on with this miserable existence.

Leo wished he were back in the cupboard under the stairs. He suddenly wished he were back listening to the grunts and the screams, even seeing the bruises afterwards. 'Black and blue' – anything was better than this.

Leo's mind wandered back to the times when his first mum, his *original* mum, had given him some love and kindness, when there was enough money, and the men didn't need to come, when there wasn't any booze in the house. Occasionally there had been some love and kindness. He was sure sometimes she had put her arms around him. It did happen, he was sure it did!

Leo then thought back to when his grandmother had been alive, and the distant memories made his eyes sting with tears and every bone in his body shake.

Grandma. The only real kindness he had ever known – walks to the park, feeding the ducks, hot baths and homemade cakes – a lifetime ago. Why did Grandma have to die!

Grandma used to shout at his mum, tell her she was 'a disgrace'. She would bundle Leo up and take him to her little bungalow, where he knew he was safe.

Leo was physically shaking so much now that he could feel his teeth chattering in his mouth. He was completely engulfed with emotion and was picking at his hands furiously.

NOBODY WANTED HIM … NOBODY AT ALL … UNWANTED, UNWANTED, UNWANTED.

Leo didn't consciously lunge forward and out of the cupboard door. Although he had been fantasising about it a few minutes before, he didn't consciously run at his 'new parents'. He was totally out of control, in a blind rage as he ran toward Ingrid with his fists clenched, and as he reached her, the speed with which he charged at her left him unable to slow down in time, and he just ran straight into her at full pace, fists still clenched. knocking her backwards … bang, flat onto her back, and he fell on top of her with a thud.

As Leo, half on top of his adoptive mother, legs draped over hers, suddenly came to his senses, he didn't know what to do next.

The room was completely silent for about five seconds, although it seemed much longer. Ingrid was still beneath him, quiet and unmoving. Leo wondered if he had knocked her out, or even killed her!

Then, slowly but surely, the commotion started. 'GET HIM OFF … EDDIE, GET HIM OFF … GET THE DIRTY

BRAT OFF ME NOW!' Ingrid's voice was shaky but loud and hysterical.

Leo felt himself being grabbed by the back of his shirt and hauled into the air by Eddie. He then realised he was being thrown toward the very cupboard he had charged out of.

Leo felt as though he had been catapulted, and then he felt himself crash through the open cupboard door and land in a heap in almost the same spot he had started from ... full circle!

Ingrid was now screeching at the top of her voice. Eddie was trying to pull her to her feet. She looked dishevelled, and Leo could see blood at the back of her head, oozing through her thin hair, probably from how he had knocked her backwards, as she had landed with the back of her head hitting the kitchen floor tiles with force.

Ingrid was screeching obscenities. Leo amazed himself by again stifling the urge to giggle. Obscenities. He knew what obscenities were – prostitute ... hooker ... whore!

Then Leo heard another word which he had heard many times before – BASTARD. Oh yes, little fuckin' bastard!

Eddie managed to pull Ingrid onto her feet, and they both half-sat and half-fell into chairs.

My Fucking Wonderful New Mother and Father, thought Leo as he peered at them from the cupboard.

His 'dad', he noticed, was very pale, almost white. His 'mum', however, was the opposite, red as a beetroot, she was, and continuing to screech.

'The feral brat needs sorting out ... the little runt ... the little BASTARD!' On and on and on, worse than he had ever heard from his *real* mother, worse than the mother who had never wanted him.

After what seemed like an eternity but was probably only a few minutes, Ingrid calmed down and reverted to a calm and cold tone as she said, 'Get to your room, you little lump of shit. I'll be ringing them damn social workers about this. Don't think you are getting away with it! Duped, we've been, Ed, bloody duped. They've fobbed us off and palmed a wild animal off on us.' As she spoke, Ingrid rubbed the cut on the back of her head with her hand.

Leo looked from her to 'Dad', and Eddie was nodding at him, an urgent nod. His face looked like he was wearing a ghost mask except there was an expression of panic about it.

Until this point, Leo hadn't realised that he was hurt. He tried to stand but one leg gave way. He felt a pain shoot through it as he tried to put weight on it. He crumpled under the pain and fell back to the floor.

Ingrid was merciless. She looked at Leo with disgust in her eyes. 'I said get to your room NOW!' she blasted.

Leo tried to stand again. His eyes filled with tears, and there was a lump in his throat, which seemed to be stopping him from swallowing. He didn't know if he was crying with physical pain or emotional pain, but his leg was throbbing, and he just knew he wouldn't make it up the stairs, so he stood there, letting his good leg bear the weight. His head felt like lead, and he didn't know want to do.

Leo heard 'Dad's' voice then, quiet and monotone, emotionless. 'I think he's hurt, Ingrid. When I threw him ...'

It was as though Eddie were talking to no-one. He wasn't looking at Ingrid; he wasn't looking at Leo. He was staring ahead, still ghostly white. He seemed as much in shock as Leo himself!

Ingrid wasn't in shock, however. No, she was angry and cold and hard.

'I don't care whether he's hurt or not. *I'm* hurt, and I didn't start this. I DONT BLOODY CARE IF HE'S HALF-DEAD, EDDIE! Get him out of here and out of my sight before I do something to him!'

Eddie rose from the table, where he was half-slumped and still, and walked slowly toward the cupboard, where Leo was trying to keep upright, holding onto the door-frame to assist him and keeping all his weight on the leg which didn't hurt.

Leo flinched as his 'Dad' reached him and made physical contact. He didn't know what to expect. Was he going to be thrown across the room again? Was he going to get a beating? Maybe he would be 'black and blue' like his real mother used to be after the men had been.

Leo flinched for a second time as his 'dad' tried to pick him up. He felt another shot of pain in his injured leg, then suddenly he was thrust over Eddie's shoulder. It wasn't rough, but it wasn't gentle, just slung over like a sack of potatoes!

Leo felt himself being carried out of the kitchen and up the stairs. It probably wasn't too much of an effort for Eddie, who was a big, portly man, and Leo was small for his eight years. Despite being in his *wonderful* new home for a few months now, he was still underweight.

When they reached his bedroom, Leo felt his 'dad' ease him down onto his bed, again not roughly but certainly not gently either, just lowering him down enough to not drop him, and then there he was, lying on his back, gazing up at Eddie with a 'What happens now?' expression.

Eddie didn't wait around to seek any form of communication with Leo. He looked a bit closer at Leo's injured leg. His trousers were ripped, and Eddie could see a gash on the side of his shin, but he didn't think it was broken or anything, so with a resigned sigh he said, 'Get into bed and go to sleep,' and then he was gone!

Leo started shaking and picking at his hands as soon as his 'dad' had left the room. He was trying to make sense of it all, the last fifteen minutes or so, if that's how long it had been.

The shaking turned to tears before long, not silent tears now but great big wracking sobs. Leo couldn't make sense of anything, anything at all.

He tried to clear his mind, to think straight. His leg was throbbing like mad and there was blood trickling from the open wound. Leo's head was swimming. It never dawned on him for one minute that he could and should tell the social worker who still visited sometimes. It never occurred to Leo in the slightest that how he was being treated was emotional harm and that tonight it had been physical harm.

Leo would never think in a million years that anyone would ever care enough to stick up for him! He expected to be blamed – after all, it was he who had charged at 'Mum' and landed on top of her, and he didn't really know why!

Leo realised, despite his young age, that he had never felt so alone in the whole of his life, not during all the nights before when the men used to come and go, hiding and praying for the screaming and the grunting to stop. No, not even then. Not like now.

Leo didn't realise that his feelings were ones of dashed hopes and dashed dreams, no Forever Family to love and cherish him. They didn't take him on for that reason!

Through the blur of events, trying to make sense of why he had charged from the cupboard, why he ran at her so angrily, the realisation *really* hit Leo. It hit him even more painfully than hearing their words earlier.

'Own agenda for taking the kid.'
'Maybe not completely honest.'
'Someone to look after Lucy.'
'Little indiscretions.'

Leo couldn't make sense of some of the things he had heard, but he knew as usual what it meant: unwanted, unwanted, unwanted!

Leo didn't, however, get the surge of emotion he had experienced in the cupboard. He couldn't have charged at anyone, even if he had wanted to. His leg was throbbing, *really* throbbing, but he had no adrenalin left in any event!

A different emotion was, however, creeping over him again. It was a calm feeling, among the feelings of being completely unlovable, alone, unwanted, tired, hurting, and distressed. Another emotion was emerging, a very strange feeling which he didn't recognise!

Leo lay straight on his bed, on his back, arms behind his head, staring up at the ceiling, the cold whitewashed bare clinical ceiling. Even the pain in his leg seemed to ease.

Was he drifting into some sort of unconsciousness? Was he dreaming? He felt like he was floating.

Little Leo, eight years old, neglected and unwanted by everyone around him, new mum, old mum – how many more mums might there be that *wouldn't* want him?

And so, there was something building up inside him, a new feeling, which made him feel a little bit better. It would be a few more months until he recognised the feeling as REVENGE.

OH YES! Leo wanted REVENGE!

'I hate this feeling, like I am here but I am not, like someone cares but they do not, like I belong somewhere else … anywhere but here.' (Research)

I am a child who knew within, a long, long time ago,
That no one really wanted me, but I live on and grow,
And when I finally get my time, to pay back all the pain,
I guess that it might be hell … when we meet again.

CHAPTER SIX

'IS BAD TRANSPARENT?' – BENEATH THE SURFACE

Things changed after the night of the cupboard incident.

Leo hadn't known what to expect. He had hardly slept a wink after 'Dad' had carried him up to bed like a sack of potatoes.

He had lain long into the night trying to understand this new feeling which was stirring inside him and unconsciously lay picking his hands and trying to rub away the throbbing in his leg.

His 'parents' (huh!), his so-called bloody parents, came nowhere near him. No-one came to see whether he was okay, whether he wanted anything to eat or drink, to see if he was still in pain from the injury to his leg. Nothing … no-one … he didn't matter … he was unwanted.

Leo had drifted into what seemed like a dream sleep some time around dawn. He had lain there for hours when he saw the light start to creep in through his window.

No-one had drawn his curtains the night before. He usually closed them himself when he put himself to bed.

As the light appeared, Leo started drifting, which he thought was the wrong way round – *you were supposed to go to sleep when it was dark*, he mused to himself as he felt his eyelids getting heavy.

He didn't sleep for long, however – maybe half an hour, maybe a little bit more.

He could hear the usual bustle of the morning routine downstairs in the kitchen.

Ingrid was heavy-footed, and she was banging around the kitchen as she always did, putting out cereal for him and making hot buttered toast for her precious Lucy.

Eddie was also quite loud that morning. He got himself ready for work next door in the 'house of the dead'.

As Leo was going over things in his mind, not knowing what to do, he wasn't even conscious that he had reverted to calling 'Mum' and 'Dad' 'Ingrid' and 'Eddie' in his mind.

He listened to the morning carrying on as if nothing had happened the night before and gently opened his bedroom door slightly.

Was it his imagination that Ingrid was banging and slamming things around the kitchen even more than usual, louder than ever? Even Eddie seemed loud, as if they were trying to cover something up.

However, whether it was his imagination or not, Leo could still hear them both going about their morning business, so what was he supposed to do? Not so brave now but hungry and tired, he decided to brave it, go downstairs and see how things were. I mean, it couldn't really get much worse, could it!

Leo left his room as quietly as he could. As he descended the stairs, he purposely tried to make a bit of noise. Subconsciously, he was trying to warn them that he was coming.

As he walked into the kitchen, he had no idea what reception was awaiting him. He felt scared. He wasn't sure why, but he was.

Leo had been through so much in his life. He had known what it was like to feel sad, lonely, scared, and unwanted for as long as he could remember, so he couldn't quite understand the feelings of fear which crept over him now.

As he walked into the kitchen, Ingrid was facing him and saw him immediately. As she did, she turned away, so that her back was facing him, and she started moving cleaning products around from the back of the sink, aimlessly, really, just picking up bottles of washing-up liquid and bleach and altering their positions in the cleaning tray completely unnecessarily.

Not a word, not a mutter, no dirty look, no mumbling or grunting toward him like she had done previously, just absolutely nothing at all.

Eddie took a different approach. He moved toward Leo with a forced smile on his face. His voice was quieter than usual as he said, 'Sit down, lad. I'll get you some breakfast.'

Leo did as he was asked and sat in his place at the table, on the smallest chair, of course, the one which had been squeezed in among the three larger ones.

There was no bowl of cereal waiting like usual. The table hadn't been laid. There was no sign of Lucy, not that that bothered him, spiteful little madam that she was, like her mother. Oh yes. Leo remembered a saying which someone had said about him once. 'The apple hasn't fallen far from the tree there.' Someone had been referring to him looking like his mother, his *real* mother, but Lucy was much more than that. She was like Ingrid in every way but in a smaller body!

Leo focused his mind back to the present, to Ingrid with her back to him, still moving cleaning products around for no good reason at all.

Leo looked at Eddie, looking through the cupboard for some cereal, clearly not used to getting breakfast ready. He found a box of Rice Krispies. He moved toward Leo and placed them down in front of him before turning back around to get a bowl, spoon, and some milk from the fridge.

Before he could finalise his task of providing Leo with a complete bowl of cereal, Leo startled him by saying, 'Why did you bring me here when you don't really want me?'

His voice was now loud, very loud, menacing, almost. He didn't recognise it himself. He sounded grown up, like a man, like an angry man, much older than his eight tender years.

Eddie spun around from where he had been rooting through the cutlery drawer for a spoon. His expression looked startled, frightened, almost!

He looked from Leo to Ingrid at the same time that Leo looked at Ingrid, just as she turned around from her meaningless task at the sink. She averted her eyes from Leo and said to Eddie, 'I told you last night, Ed, I'm having nothing to do with IT any more, nothing at all. You can send IT back for all I care, IT's not worth it; the brat is bad through and through.'

As Ingrid's response dawned on Leo, he realised he was the 'IT', and he started to laugh. It was not a childish laugh, which one might expect from a young child. No, oh no. It was a loud, raucous, cynical laugh, once again making him sound much older than his years.

Ingrid, horrible, nasty, vicious Ingrid, was referring to him in terms he had been referred to all his life. Very rarely had he been called by his name, as if he didn't have one!

Eddie was looking at Leo with real fear now. *Fear of what?* thought Leo. Fear of what he might do? Or fear of what he might say next?

It was laughable, really laughable, thought Leo, these two larger-than-life adults looking at him the way they were – Ingrid with disdain, almost ambivalent, and yet he sensed the unease within her.

Eddie now just looked petrified, and Leo felt that feeling return, that feeling of something nice, something in his favour for once … POWER.

He repeated his question, his face directed at Eddie, his chin slightly tilted up, making his little pixie face look almost defiant.

'I ASKED YOU, why did you bring me here when you don't really want me?' Still no answer.

'DIDN'T YOU HEAR ME? DIDN'T YOU FUCKIN' HEAR ME? I SAID … WHY DID YOU BRING ME HERE WHEN YOU DONT REALLY WANT ME?

I heard you last night. You never really wanted me. It's all lies, all fuckin' lies, fuckin' lies, lies, lies!'

Leo thought that maybe Eddie was going to collapse. He had turned as white as a sheet again and seemed to be trembling.

Leo felt his power surging. He had no idea how he made his voice change, no idea at all, but somewhere in the back of his mind, somewhere dark and frightening, he remembered voices, just like the voice which was coming from him now. He blocked that particular memory out … he had to.

There was so much which Leo didn't understand; he was eight years old, for God's sake. However, eight years old, small for his age but presently with a grown-up menacing voice, which was scaring the hell out of his great big gorm-less bloody adopted father!

Leo looked from Eddie's pale face to Ingrid. She too seemed to be in shock but nowhere near as much as Eddie. She was more composed and once again looked through Leo and addressed her husband.

'Stop IT shouting and swearing, and get IT out of here, Ed. I am warning you – ring the bloody social worker now. I mean it. That demon feral brat is not staying in this house a moment longer,' she spat.

'Demon' … 'feral'. These were new words to Leo, and he was sure they were not complimentary.

Eddie seemed to compose himself a little. Nonetheless, his voice was shaking as he said, 'Leave things to me, Ingrid. Go and see to Lucy. I'll sort the lad out.'

Ingrid wasn't giving in that easily, however. 'I said IT's not staying in this house a moment longer,' she said more forcefully now, but to Leo's surprise, Eddie still came back at her.

'Okay, Ingrid, but for now, off you go and let me deal with things.'

Leo didn't know or understand that Eddie may have come across as patronising toward Ingrid, but he did know that Ingrid was not going to like Eddie's insistence.

He looked from one to the other, and suddenly it was like he wasn't there at all. 'IT' … 'feral brat' … the cause of all of this, like he wasn't even there. It was now a bat-tle of wills between two people who, actually, deep down and with some honesty, were two people who probably didn't like each other very much!

Leo's eyes darted between them, eager, almost like an animal ready to pounce.

Ingrid was looking at Eddie, and her feelings were not hidden now. She gave him a look which was very meaningful before she turned and left the kitchen, leaving a cold presence where she had been.

Leo looked at Eddie as Ingrid left, and if he were n't so consumed with this new feeling of power, he might almost have felt sorry for him!

Eddie decided to change his approach, and his voice took on more of a pleading tone as he said to Leo, 'Go and get ready for school, lad. Try not to worry. We'll need to talk about your bad language and behaviour later, but you need to get to school now.'

'I'M NOT GOING TO SCHOOL!' bellowed Leo, the grown-up voice resurfacing, the feelings of power surging through him like something hot and bubbling.

Eddie's face returned to being pale, paler even than before, if that were possible!

What was he to do now? It was like the boy had changed from the quiet, withdrawn child he had been yesterday into some type of raging monster. Was it temper tantrums? Was it normal for a kid with his background?

It was pretty scary, thought Eddie. Then again, it was pretty scary when Lucy had temper tantrums, he told himself. However, he knew it wasn't the same, not the same at all!

Lucy was spoilt, very spoilt, and always had been, but this was different on a different level.

Eddie then rationalised that the boy hadn't had a chance in life so far. There were bound to be teething problems and issues. His life had been chaotic, abusive, and neglectful.

Eddie turned back to look at Leo. If he were completely honest with himself, he had grown fond of the lad, but Ingrid saw him as a means to an end, or at least she had. Now she just wanted him to go back!

A stronger man, a better man, thought Eddie to himself, would have made a stand about how the lad had been treated from the start. It was just an existence, really, probably better than what he had been used to, but not really much of a life!

It couldn't have been more than a minute or two in between Leo bellowing that he 'wasn't going to school' and Eddie trying to address this with him again, but during that minute or two, so many things flashed through Eddie's mind that he thought he might be going mad. He thought he might be having his own life flash before him for a reason.

His life, his miserable life, meeting Ingrid, believing briefly that she was bubbly and full of fun, definitely the girl for him, and then realising soon after they were married that she could be cold and manipulative and that her all-consuming obsession to have a child would take precedence above anything else in their lives – no more fun, no more laughter!

Eddie cast his mind back to the period of time when he had used prostitutes and she had found out. He struggled to recall how she had treated him then, how bad it had got!

Then Lucy was born, and things were good for a while until Ingrid's obsession with her became overbearing, never being able to say no, wanting Lucy to always have the best of everything, even when it financially crippled them.

Eddie had tears in his eyes when he thought of his beautiful darling daughter, so innocent, so unspoiled when born, and now the very double of her mother.

She was still beautiful, still his little girl, of course, but spoilt, selfish, and demanding, and though his mind half-refuted what he was thinking, Eddie knew in his heart that Lucy was already calculating and spiteful!

Then his mind turned back to the lad, this little boy, who had been born into poverty and neglect, seemingly wanted by no-one and then landing on their doorstep after a few months of an adoption assessment.

He thought about how Ingrid and he had hatched a plan to provide Lucy with a sibling, a companion for when they were old and gone.

Looking back, as Eddie stood in the kitchen a few feet from the subject of their devious planning, he realised it had been a bloody stupid idea in the first place, one of Ingrid's 'I am right, and you won't stop me' ideas!

And here they were, in charge of a child they hadn't wanted for the right reasons, a child who had experienced a terrible start in life and who needed love and affection, but what were they giving him? It wasn't love and affection, was it? A place around the table, barely, squashed in like an afterthought, cereal for breakfast, a school lunch, sandwich for dinner, homework and bed!

A wave of shame wafted over Eddie, and he almost felt pain from it. All the different emotions he had ever felt in his life paled into insignificance. Here was this boy, this tiny boy, struggling to find some sort of control in a world which had done nothing but inflict misery on him.

No wonder he was struggling and reacting. No wonder he was angry and starting to be defiant!

And at that moment, everything changed. Absolutely everything changed, and none of their lives would ever be the same again.

So, it had taken a minute, maybe two, long enough for Eddie to have a rude awakening and to be ashamed, thoroughly ashamed of the reasons they had wanted to adopt this poor boy and how his life had been since he had come to them.

Eddie's insight was the miracle Leo needed, because insight comes with empathy, and empathy can lead to love. This was the moment which changed Leo's life for the better, briefly, for how could Eddie or he have known or predicted that it was already too late, that the cruel hand of fate was already working against them!

Leo was apprehensive as Eddie moved towards him. For a minute he wondered whether Eddie was going to strike him as he edged toward him with a strange look on his face.

Leo was then shocked when Eddie said in a kind voice, 'It's okay, Leo. You don't have to go to school today. You're upset, and things aren't your fault. Things are going to change around here. Go and get your clothes on and we'll go to the park, and we can get an ice cream.'

The tone of Eddie's voice completely threw Leo off course. He had planned to carry on refusing, to shout, to scream, to lunge, to kick, to spit, whatever it took to feel that feeling of *control* and *power*, and then *revenge*!

Now, he just crumpled. All the previous energy just drained from him, and he sat back in his chair at the table, put his head in his hands and cried and cried!

Eddie lifted Leo up, not like previously, which had felt awkward and uncaring, but much more gently now. He encouraged Leo to place his head on his shoulder, and he carried him upstairs and into his bedroom.

Leo didn't resist. He really was in a confused state now – no school, the promise of the park and an ice cream, and the distant thought of his grandmother were all entwined with his present thoughts of confusion at Eddie's change of behaviour.

'Get dressed, Leo,' Eddie said calmly. 'I'll meet you downstairs in ten minutes. Ingrid will have to take any work calls this morning; it won't hurt her. Come on, lad, it's all going to be okay.'

And so, things changed, just like that!

Leo became part of the family and was treated with love and care, but only by Eddie! There had, of course, been the initial reaction from Ingrid, closely followed by protests from Lucy and then the pattern which followed.

Leo heard the arguments, Ingrid shouting that she would leave, crying and sobbing followed by trying to manipulate Eddie to do things her way. 'You're making him more important than Lucy!' she yelled. 'It wasn't supposed to be like this; he's taking over the house!'

Leo felt grateful for being called 'him' and 'he'. It was better than 'it' or 'brat'!

Dad, as Leo now thought of Eddie, always called him Leo now, since things had changed. There was a new kindness and sort of caring which reminded him of his grandmother, not the same but a bit like it!

The arguments between Eddie and Ingrid went on for a few weeks, and each time Leo worried that things might go back to how they had been, Dad becoming disinterested again and a bowl of cereal in the morning and a sandwich at night.

But things didn't revert, and although Leo couldn't understand it, Dad seemed to get stronger, seemed more able to have a voice and stand up to Ingrid.

'It's up to you,' he would say to her when she made one of her many threats to leave. "I'm not telling you to leave, Ingrid, but I won't try and stop you. This house and the business have been in my family for years. I'll be staying put whatever you choose to do, and I'm telling you straight, Leo is now part of this family and my God, that was your doing, wasn't it?'

And so, it continued, Eddie ensuring that Leo had some quality of life, some love and care, and he felt satisfied as he saw Leo start to gain confidence, not in anger and control but in a pleasing way – little jokes here and there, some banter! He had made some friends at school as well and was socialising more.

Eddie ate with Leo every evening, and they chatted about how their days had been.

Eddie was surprised at how interested Leo was in the business. He reminded Eddie of himself at that age. *Must be a 'boy' thing*, he thought.

However, he wasn't sure that too many kids would take an interest in how dead bodies were preserved before burial or cremation, how they were embalmed, and how to act in a certain way in front of grieving relatives – calmly and respectfully!

But Leo was fascinated by the family business, just like Eddie had been as a child. He was intrigued and interested, and whenever he got the chance he was by Eddie's side in the funeral parlour.

He didn't mind that there were dead bodies – the dead can't hurt you! Leo liked the calmness, the feeling of peace, and, of course, the cleanliness of it all.

The workshop was spotless, of course, a *must* for a successful undertaker's business. No-one wanted to leave their precious dead relatives anywhere dirty.

Leo also enjoyed the time he got to spend with Eddie – Dad. It was like he was a real dad all of a sudden, and time in the funeral parlour was like father-and-son time, a father showing his son all about the family business and teaching him the ropes!

Eddie told Leo that the business would be his one day. That always made him shiver. He wasn't sure whether it was the thought of what sort of business it was or the thought that he, Leo, the kid nobody wanted, would inherit something one day, but it filled him with excitement in any event!

Leo suddenly belonged and had a future!

Eddie questioned himself at times. Leo wasn't yet nine years old, and yet Eddie was teaching him all about dead bodies and funerals and how to change his behaviour to suit the sober mood which was par for the course.

However, that was how it was, and that was how it continued. The family was divided, Ingrid and Lucy pampering themselves at every opportunity – nights in front of the TV together, hot chocolate with marshmallows, dance lessons, pony riding, piano tutorials – nothing was too much trouble or expense for Lucy.

Ingrid still regularly threatened to leave and take Lucy with her, but the threats fell on deaf ears, and Ingrid knew her power had been diluted. If she left, it would be to rent a small property somewhere, and while she knew that Eddie would provide for Lucy, it would be very different from the indulgent lifestyle which they both presently enjoyed.

So, the threats became fewer, and Ingrid, like all bullies, backed off once her power and dominance had no effect. She took what she could get. She helped herself to the family's finances whenever she wanted, oh yes. It was a profitable business, that of the dead, very profitable, and this hadn't escaped Ingrid when she had first met Eddie. It hadn't escaped her at all!

And so that was how life played out that summer, Ingrid and Lucy living life however they chose and Eddie and Leo developing a bond over the love of dead bodies and the family business, happy just to be left alone to do so!

The months passed. The social workers rarely visited, only now and then. In August there was a flurry of activity. Two social workers visited in quick succession. Eddie was filling in lots of forms and answering lots of questions, and then Leo was told,

'Well, Leo, lad,' said Eddie one morning at the beginning of September, 'the adoption order is about to be made. You will legally belong to our family forever.'

Leo didn't know how he felt about this news. They had not sat down as a family and rejoiced at this, of course. It had just been Dad telling him after the second social worker had visited. She had stayed for ages. She had asked him a few questions then spent time with Ingrid and Dad. When she left, Ingrid and Lucy went out without a word!

Leo and Dad were in the funeral parlour. Dad had some paperwork to complete, and he was going to polish the new coffins which had just been delivered. He loved doing that. It was his favourite job, making the wood all shiny and the brass handles glow!

Cardboard coffins were apparently the new trend, and Dad had dealt with a couple of funerals of this kind, but Leo loved seeing the lovely wooden ones, the ones he could clean and polish and pretend he'd made himself.

So, that was it. On a relatively warm summery day in September, the adoption order was made.

No fuss, no big party. There was no 'celebration hearing', which Leo had been told might happen.

Dad simply went to court, and a judge kindly put his wig on Leo's head, and everyone laughed.

The judge said it was a pleasure to make the adoption order, and Leo's birth certificate would now be changed to have the same name as his 'Forever Family' – Leo Twigg!

Leo learned that his birth mother now no longer had any parental rights over him at all. *What a laugh*, he thought to himself cynically. She had just lost all rights over a kid she had never wanted in the first place. He wondered if she knew, if anyone had made contact and told her. Well, that should make her day!

One of the social workers whom he had seen briefly over the eleven months he had lived with his new family was at the court hearing. She smiled at Leo, a satisfied smile as she shook Dad's hand and congratulated him.

Leo heard his dad say, 'Ingrid is heartbroken that she can't be here for this special occasion.' He lied!

'She's feeling so unwell and didn't want anything to detract from this amazing day.' He lied again!

79

The social worker looked at Eddie with a strange but knowing look. She then looked at Leo, this little boy whom she and her colleagues had talked about in the office sometimes.

'Poor kid had a terrible start. The adopters seem okay, run of the mill … he seems warmer in his approach than her. We've tried everything to trace the birth mother; not a single response. Probably doesn't want to be found! No birth father identified.'

The social worker now looked at this adoptive dad smiling down on his new legal son, then she looked at Leo, still small for his age, not so thin, not so nervy any more, not picking at his hands now.

It was very strange that the adoptive mother wasn't here. The social worker had never known it happen before – who would miss such an event! They could have changed the date if she was that sick, and where was the adoptive sister? Why hadn't the dad brought the adoptive sister along to celebrate her new brother?

Oh well, the social worker wasn't going to dwell on things. Despite the visits over the last few months seeming strained, 'Something *not* quite right,' she had said to her colleagues, with a big case load of children in all sorts of situations – fostered, living in children's homes, living at risk, etcetera – she couldn't be expected to explore an adoption case in depth, could she?

What could go wrong? The boy had no-one else in the world. The adopters had been approved by a professional panel. It was all good. No time for niggles or gut feelings, she told herself as she wished Eddie and Leo 'all the very best for the future'.

JOB DONE … ADOPTION SUCCESSFUL … CASE CLOSED!

'New beginnings are often disguised
as painful endings.'
(Research)

CHAPTER 7

'GOOD OR BAD' – NEARLY WANTED

So, Leo was adopted. He belonged. He was wanted, at least by Eddie – 'Dad'!

The night after he and Dad had gone to court, Leo had heard Eddie and Ingrid arguing again – nothing unusual there!

It was different this time. Ingrid wasn't threatening to leave. She wasn't giving her usual speech of, 'I'll take Lucy somewhere where you will never clap eyes on her again, Ed.'

No, this time Ingrid was screeching something about Eddie's *will*. 'Adopting that brat legally had better not change your will in respect of Lucy,' she screeched.

Eddie had, however, found a new way to stick up for himself with Ingrid, and he did so now. 'Lucy will always be provided for, don't you worry about that.' He purposely did *not* say, 'And so will you, Ingrid,' because he had learned recently to understand her manipulative behaviours and had learned that usually her questions and demands were focused on Lucy but that actually they were about herself!

Yes, Lucy was the centre of their world, and yes, Ingrid did have a hold on Eddie like no other because of that. But what about Leo? He had to matter as well, and Eddie had found himself warming more and more to the boy with every passing day.

The boy reminded him of himself so much, it was canny! At least the bloody social workers got that bit right when they did their 'matching' – the link between adopters and children, where they try to find similarities. They must have seen some likeness. Leo didn't look *unlike* him, he supposed, except Eddie was a large man and Leo was small.

The social workers probably didn't think much about matching, he thought cynically. They wanted a child. Leo needed a home. Eddie doubted that there was much more to it than that!

So, as late September and early October passed, Leo's birthday and the one-year anniversary of him coming to live with his adopters approached – HALLOWEEN!

Leo continued to show an almost unhealthy interest in the family business. He learned that there were three names for the job which Dad did.

One was 'undertaker', a word which had been used since the 1400s. It did not originally stem from the fact that undertakers placed bodies underground. It was designed to name a person who would 'undertake a task', usually associated with wood-working.

Undertakers could build a house, a cabinet, or a coffin for you, until the term later became a specific name for someone taking care of the deceased!

Leo soaked this information up like a sponge. His questions were endless, and Eddie was happy to share and educate his new son.

For a period of time, Eddie felt more settled, more fulfilled than he had in a long time, naively believing that everything was okay, despite Leo's terrible early days and despite Ingrid and Lucy practically ignoring that he even existed!

Leo learned about the second name for his dad's job through asking more questions. 'Where does the word 'mortician' come from, Dad?' he enquired one morning.

Here we go, thought Eddie, not unkindly. '"Mortician" comes from the Latin word "mort", which means "death",' he told his son, who listened intently.

'It doesn't tend to be used much any more.'

'Oh, okay,' said Leo. 'So, why aren't you called a funeral director, Dad?'

Leo was referring to the sign outside the front door, which said, 'EDWARD TWIGG – FUNERAL DIRECTOR, FAMILY-RUN BUSINESS SINCE 1922'.

'Well,' said Eddie, still patient with Leo's never-ending questions, 'the "funeral director" part of my job refers to the fact that I arrange the funerals, whereas the "undertaker" part of my job now refers to the preparing of the bodies and placing them in the ground or arranging cremation.

Things have changed over the years, lad.' Eddie was wistful. Leo listened intently.

'People see the two things differently. They see one as the arrangements and the other as the preparing of the body.'

Leo's ears really pricked up. He really did have an interest in the preparing of the bodies. 'Can you tell me more about the embalming, Dad?' he persisted.

'Leo, I have told you before, you are not old enough to know that stuff! I make them look nice for their families to see them one last time and to say goodbye.'

'How?' pushed Leo.

'Leo,' Eddie's voice was stern now, 'you are young; much too young. I was sixteen before my father even allowed me to know that bodies need preparing ahead of a funeral.'

Leo knew it wasn't worth pushing the conversation any further. Dad was adamant, and so he carried on with his job of polishing the shiny handles on the sides of the new coffins.

Leo knew from the conversations he had overheard – the conversations he wasn't supposed to listen to – that things were changing on the burial and cremation front, and more and more people were opting for cardboard coffins. 'It won't make a difference to business,' he had heard Dad tell Ingrid when she had grilled him about it.

Leo was practiced in the art of listening to conversations he wasn't supposed to hear. It was the benefit of his early days, he thought to himself, only having one parent who didn't give a shit about what he heard!

He heard Ingrid barking questions at Eddie. 'Will you still charge the maximum price? Will you still offer finance deals to make sure you get over the odds?'

Even at his young age, Leo took this to mean that Ingrid had no care or regard for people who were probably struggling to pay for a funeral for loved ones, people who were grieving and devastated at their loss. Leo had seen such people, when he shouldn't have, crying and sobbing while Dad comforted them and tried to offer support.

Eddie knew it was a myth that cardboard coffins were cheaper than wooden ones, although you would expect that they would be. Grieving relatives could still choose as simple or as extravagant a coffin as they wished.

Cardboard coffins could be so personal, Eddie had thought when they first came on the market. Any personal pictorial or background setting could be printed onto them, and, of course, they were much more eco-friendly.

Leo was not as keen. He loved the wooden coffins with the brass handles, which he could polish until they gleamed.

You wouldn't need to polish cardboard, would you? Leo smiled to himself as if amused, wondering how he would clean them.

He doubted it would be with soap and water, although he had heard Dad say that they were designed to withstand water.

He could try throwing a bucket of water over them. Leo smiled to himself again, but he really would miss the wooden coffins if these cardboard things took off!

Surely cardboard coffins must either be genius for the future or the worst idea ever!

He wondered how cardboard could be strong enough to hold a dead body, but he had heard Dad say that they could hold up to twenty-three, stone! *That was a lot of weight*, thought Leo, who was small and thin still.

Eddie remembered thinking the same thing when he had completed his research. He hoped these coffins could hold weight and withstand water, or there was likely to be some highly publicised nightmare stories hitting the press, and he didn't want any of that nonsense!

Eddie wondered for the hundredth time why Leo was so interested in the business and all which went with it. He certainly was a quirky kid, no doubt about that!

Later that afternoon, as Leo was helping with the coffins, Eddie told him it was time to go back into the house. He had jobs to do which Leo wasn't allowed to see or know about.

Leo wanted to protest, because he knew exactly what his dad was about to do. He had watched him one afternoon when he was supposed to be in his bedroom. Ingrid had been out with Lucy, and Leo had taken the opportunity to hide behind the screens which were regularly used to protect the modesty of the dead bodies.

Leo had been fascinated that afternoon. He could barely breathe as he watched his dad at work … embalming a body!

Leo had felt a chill in the air that afternoon despite it being warm, and he was excited by the sight of the dead body which Dad was working on!

He had had to be very careful about his excitement, had to stifle the gasps he wanted to make, had to remain perfectly still so that his dad didn't know he was there. The years of practice in the cupboard had helped, he was sure.

Eddie had no idea that Leo had seen things he should not have seen, had watched him plug in the embalming machine, watched him unwrap the dead body out of the ice it had been transported in to preserve it.

Eddie would have been more than mortified had he known that Leo had watched him drain the blood from the body, replacing it with the embalming fluid, making the body look better the minute the fluid entered the carotid artery – a bit waxy, maybe, but *much* better.

As Leo watched, Eddie then had to complete the dead body's make-up!

It had taken Eddie two years in 'mortuary school' just to be able to put make-up on dead bodies!

Ingrid had joked about that in the early days. 'Blimey,' she had laughed out loud, 'I learned to do my make-up without a teacher!'

When the job was complete, Eddie had placed a piece of plastic over the late woman's face to stop the make-up from smudging and to stop any dust landing on it.

And all the while, Leo had watched from behind the screens, fascinated by the whole thing, far more fascinated than any eight-year-old should be in such circumstances. Maybe he didn't realise the concept of death or the finality of it!

On this afternoon, however, Leo knew there was no way he could hide and watch again, as Ingrid was home, and she always knew exactly when Eddie was preparing to embalm and 'titillate' a body – her word.

Although Leo knew that Ingrid couldn't care less about him, she took pleasure in making sure that he 'did as he was told', so it would be an afternoon spent in his bedroom today, thinking and imagining Dad and the machine which drained the blood, and the embalming fluid which plumped the body out again!

He would imagine the make-up which made the dead face look alive again, and he would get excited at the thought of death, although he did not know why!

The day before Leo's ninth birthday was a cold, wet, and windy day. There hadn't been many 'trick-or-treaters' so far, probably because kids didn't want to venture out in such miserable weather conditions.

There was still plenty of evidence of the Halloween season, however. Houses were decorated with witches and ghosts, pretend skeleton bones were eerily planted in front gardens, and carved pumpkins were lit up by candles in porches and front windows.

Occasionally, some cheeky kid would shout out as he passed the house and the adjoining funeral director's, 'House of the dead, house of the dead!' before scampering away feeling brave!

On the day of his ninth birthday, Halloween 2019, Leo woke feeling the same as every other day.

It was a Thursday, but there was no school, because it was half-term. As daylight and full consciousness spread over him, Leo felt lots of different emotions, but he couldn't understand what they were.

He remembered his mum, his *real* mum, the mum who never wanted him, and anger flooded him until he felt like a raging bull, ready to explode, ready to hurt someone.

He remembered, after being reminded by Dad yesterday, that he had lived here for a year now, a year with his Forever Family. This also made him angry today. A 'Forever Family' – what family? Ingrid and Lucy didn't give a shit about him!

Dad seemed to care, but was that enough? Was this how families were? Divided, tense, arguments over money, arguments over Lucy, arguments over him, the kid, the brat … unwanted! No, Leo did not wake up with happy feelings on this day at all!

Eddie had asked Leo what he would like for his birthday and what he would like to do. Leo had heard him and Ingrid arguing again. 'For God's sake, Ingrid, can you just plan a little party or something? Just some sandwiches and cakes and a few of his school friends?'

Ingrid had learned to be cool and ambivalent toward Eddie now. Screaming at him for her own way had stopped working once the 'kid' had got his feet under the table. So, she was calm and measured in her response now. 'I've told you a hundred times, Eddie, the brat is nothing to do with me. HE IS NOT NORMAL. HE IS AN EVIL CHILD, and I did not want to keep him, so I am having NOTHING to do with him. Do I make myself clear?'

Before Eddie could reply, Ingrid turned away from him with one last retort, one last low blow.

'And anyway, he hasn't got any friends. You saw the end-of-term report, didn't you? Anxious attachments, emotionally devoid, unable to form relationships with either peers or adults – I rest my case.' And on that she turned and left the kitchen, where the argument had started, yet again!

Leo didn't care that Ingrid wouldn't arrange a party for him. He didn't want a party!

It was true that he didn't have any friends. The slight progress he had made in his social skills had quickly deteriorated again. Leo didn't realise that this was probably linked to living in a family which felt like a warzone, living in a family of four, where only one other person threw him any crumb of kindness!

Leo just knew that he was different. He had always been different, but he didn't know why – probably because his own mother, his *real* mother, had never wanted him!

Happy bloody birthday, he thought to himself, emotions racing!

'A silent cry, a hungry child … emotions that were stunted, When I was born, I was not bad, but I knew I was unwanted.'

CHAPTER 8

'BAD DEED TO GOOD' –
NOT JUST ANYBODY

Eddie woke up on Halloween, and a strange sense of foreboding washed over him.

He put it down to the ongoing farce which was his marriage! Ingrid, once passionate and tempting, was now cold, callous, and demanding! My God, she was as hard as nails when it came to the boy!

Then there was Lucy, his pretty, adored, beautiful little girl, showing signs of spitefulness at such a young age, and then there was Leo, poor Leo, the unwanted kid they had taken on for their own benefit, Leo, who stuck out like a sore thumb as one of life's 'problem kids' but whom he was determined to do right by now!

As he showered, his mood lightened. He had bought Leo a drone for his birthday. Eddie hoped he would take an interest in it, because much as he liked the fact that the boy loved being in the workshop, took pride in polishing coffins and learning about the trade, it wasn't right. He was too young!

It had all started as a way of keeping the boy out from under Ingrid's feet, but now it was like he couldn't get him interested in anything else – questions about funerals; what were shrouds? Where did bodies go next? Questions about coffins, questions, questions, questions, his face lighting up at every little bit of new information!

What was it about the boy? Was it wrong? Did it show morbidness, an unhealthy interest in the dead?

Eddie had learned through his mortuary science degree that there was a stigma which came with working in this industry. People assumed that you must be dark and reclusive, 'fucked up' to want to work with dead people, but that simply wasn't the case!

Eddie knew that every time he brushed knots out of dead people's hair or painted their nails before crossing their arms across their chests, that this was the only job he could ever do. Born into it or not, he took pride in it, enjoyed it, particularly when grieving families were then pleased with his services.

He wasn't a 'vulture', a 'creepy old man' waiting for people to die! He was kind and respectful, he was sure he was, and the boy was *so* like him! Funny really, it had only been a year and yet he was *so* like him!

Eddie decided he would give Leo the best birthday he could!

There was a Halloween event in the church hall later. Maybe Leo would enjoy going to that, although Eddie knew as he had the thought that he was kidding himself!

If it were real ghosts and ghouls then Leo might be interested, but a dressing-up party where he would be expected to join in and socialise would not be Leo's cup of tea at all!

The day began and then continued the same as any other, with Leo helping Eddie polish coffins and do odd jobs around the workshop.

Eddie was trying to be positive about Leo's birthday, telling him he could choose whatever takeaway meal he fancied later, although he doubted Ingrid or Lucy would join in. It was a very different story to Lucy's birthday parties, which saw no holding back from Ingrid – balloons, personalised cakes, bouncy castles – there was even a pony dressed as a unicorn last year!

As Eddie's already sombre mood flickered between sad thoughts for this lost little boy, with all his quirks and attachment difficulties, and then all the happy times spent with Lucy, he found himself being slightly irritated when the phone in the small office at the back of the workshop started ringing.

'Leo, carry on giving those handles a good rub, and don't touch anything else. I'll be back in a tick.'

As soon as Eddie's back was turned, however, Leo seized his moment to sneak around the privacy screens and take a look.

He was disappointed – no open coffins, no dead bodies to look at. It didn't seem as though Dad was working on any bodies today. Maybe undertakers preferred not to work on Halloween. He smiled at this thought!

As Eddie ended the call, Leo saw this and scuttled back to where he was supposed to be, polishing handles and brass plaques belonging to the coffins which had yet to have dead owners placed into them. Anybody ... 'any body'. He laughed at his own joke!

Eddie looked thoughtful as he returned to the main workshop. He knew what Ingrid would have said if she had just taken that call, not that she bothered doing much to help with the business these days.

Eddie had just agreed to a request from the local priest, although he knew there would not be much money in it. *Not everything is about money*, he told himself, and he realised that he was changing, mellowing since he had tried to understand Leo's plight.

Going through the adoption process and later realising that not all children had happy childhoods had certainly taught him things, so he had just listened to the priest, whom he barely knew, and his request to receive a body which was presently at the city hospital, unclaimed and to all intents and purposes unwanted!

The priest had told him that the hospital had kept the body past the legal timeframe required, preserved on a cold slab in a refrigerator in the hospital mortuary.

The priest confirmed that some local people, mostly down-and-outs, had implied that they knew the woman vaguely. They didn't want to be involved, however.

The priest had held a collection and raised a few hundred pounds. Eddie had felt a pang when he had heard that. He doubted that the local community would donate much for such a cause, but from what he knew of the priest's reputation, he had probably supplemented the collection heavily himself.

'Is it enough?' the priest had asked Eddie.

'It depends on what you want, Father,' Eddie had replied.

Eddie was trying to sound respectful. The hospital had agreed to transport the body to him, so it would mean keeping it overnight, providing the most economical coffin available and transport to the crematorium tomorrow.

Eddie breathed deeply. He had done a few like this before over the years – a poor dead unwanted person, a whole life behind them and no-one to care about them after death!

The cremation would probably be basically a 'pauper's funeral', and then the priest would agree where to scatter the ashes afterwards.

Eddie knew the priest's collection would barely cover the cost, but as the priest continued, Eddie realised that he wasn't talking about an elderly person, as Eddie had first imagined. The priest was not talking about a person whose family had moved away and forgotten about them. No, the priest was describing a young woman in her thirties, no age at all, and no-one had come forward to identify her!

Eddie could hear the sorrow and the pity in the priest's voice as he said, 'No suspicious circumstances, just found dead in her dingy flat; prostitute they think; postmortem said heart failure.'

Eddie knew instinctively then that he would do the job and accept whatever money the priest could offer.

The word 'prostitute' sent shivers through him, not because of the priest's bluntness in using the word but because of his own little indiscretions years ago, which Ingrid had never let him forget!

And so, he agreed. The body would be arriving at four thirty p.m., a bit annoying, as Eddie had wanted an early finish to try and make a special tea for Leo's birthday, but at least he would only need to receive the body, place it in a basic budget coffin, and that would be it! No embalming, make-up, or hairstyling for an unidentified unwanted body! No grieving relatives to comfort, and no photographs! This one wouldn't take long. Very sad!

As Eddie confirmed the arrangements with the priest and ended the call, he hovered for a second, consumed again with feelings of foreboding, but he couldn't understand why; probably pity, he concluded.

On the other end of the phone, the kindly priest wondered to himself about the local undertaker, Eddie Twigg.

He had a bit of a reputation for being a stand-offish, burly type of man with a dominating wife, by all accounts.

Some would say they weren't the type of couple to support people during the grieving process, but he seemed okay, almost kindly, and the priest knew enough about funerals to know that Mr Twigg wouldn't be making much money from their agreement, so fair play, that was good of him.

The priest also remembered that the Twiggs had adopted a child last year, a deprived and neglected child, by all accounts, so they must be good people. One should never judge!

As Eddie returned to the workshop, Leo was still conscientiously polishing brass handles. That boy, he looked in his element, he did. Polishing coffins on your ninth birthday – you really couldn't make it up!

Eddie wondered what the social workers would say if they saw this picture. Polishing coffins wasn't really a part of the adoption deal, but all that was over and done with now. It really seemed like Leo was at his happiest in this workshop. It still made Eddie wonder if it was right, however.

Leo was 'his' son legally. Eddie never thought 'our' son, because he knew that Ingrid had never taken to the boy, and that was an understatement. Even before the night of the cupboard incident, when Leo seemed to lose his mind for a few minutes, she hadn't taken to him at all. She hadn't even tried!

How would it all work out? Eddie wondered. It was like walking on eggshells all the time!

At four p.m., Eddie told Leo it was time to go back into the house. There were just a few more things he had to finish, he had said, and then he would join Leo in the kitchen, and they could decide on tonight's take-away birthday meal.

Leo didn't protest, although he wanted to. He wanted to know what Dad had to do in the workshop. There were no bodies in, no-one to embalm and titillate! But he knew by now when his dad meant it, and Ingrid was in the house, so hiding and watching wasn't an option today.

The body of the young woman, which no-one had claimed or wanted, arrived at four forty p.m., ten minutes late.

The two hospital porters who carried it from the small white hospital van into the funeral parlour said nothing. They simply placed the body bag on the trolley behind the curtains as Eddie had gestured them to do, then they turned and left, still saying nothing.

Maybe they didn't know what to say, Eddie thought to himself. This probably wasn't in their everyday job description – 'DELIVER ONE DEAD AND UNWANTED YOUNG WOMAN TO THE UNDERTAKER'S.'

After they had left, Eddie set about his business. He lifted the coffin he had chosen onto the wheels which were used to push the coffins around. He pushed it through the curtains until it was adjacent to the body bag, and then he sighed as he prepared to unzip the bag and see the unfortunate corpse which no-one cared about.

The coffin wasn't the cheapest one which Eddie's firm offered. He wasn't sure what had come over him. Maybe it was the humbleness of the priest, or maybe it was the plight of the boy, but he upgraded to a more lavish coffin than the two-hundred-pounds budget one.

He certainly wouldn't make any money out of this job now. God! Ingrid would go mad if she knew.

As Eddie unzipped the bag which held the woman's body. He didn't know what to expect. 'A prostitute,' the priest had said but not unkindly.

There may be evidence of drug use, thought Eddie. He had known that many times. Maybe signs of jaundice, if in life if she had been a drinker. Maybe dirty hair, dirty nails, sunken eyes.

Eddie was prepared for any of the above as he pulled on the last part of the zip and the bag opened and parted either side of the woman's body.

Eddie wasn't, however, prepared for what he saw next as he looked down on the face of the dead woman. HE WAS NOT PREPARED AT ALL!

His legs turned to jelly, he started to shake, really shake uncontrollably, and he jumped backwards in shock!

As he stumbled backwards and sank into the coffins which lay behind him, the force of his body caused a couple of the coffins to slide backwards from where they lay neatly on large shelving.

Eddie didn't notice. Usually, he was precious about his stock of coffins, just as Leo was enthusiastic about polishing them, but right now, Eddie was cowering among them as if the dead body he had just viewed were still alive and about to jump out of the body bag and grab him!

Eddie sat for about five minutes, half-perched against a shelf and half-leaning over a coffin. His breathing was erratic, and he was in shock at what he had seen.

After a few minutes, he tried to compose himself. Should he shout for Ingrid? He contemplated it and then realised what a stupid idea that was!

What should he do? What should he do? He couldn't think straight. All sorts of ideas were running through his head. Maybe he could ring the priest and say that he couldn't commit to the job after all!

He could say that he didn't have any spare coffins, or that one of the hearses had broken down and he couldn't get the body to the crematorium tomorrow!

As Eddie's mind boggled with ridiculous thoughts, looking for any excuse which would mean someone would come and take that body away from here, he knew he was on his own in this! No-one was going to come and deal with things for him, no-one was going to understand, and so for the first time ever in his life, Eddie felt completely and utterly alone.

As his shaking calmed a little bit, Eddie began to think a little clearer. He knew he wasn't ready to go back to her body and do what he had to do, but he stood up and unconsciously straightened the coffins which he had disturbed and then made his way slowly to the office, where he kept a bottle of Scotch in a drawer in his desk.

Eddie wasn't a big drinker, or a regular one, but there were times when this line of work could be overwhelming, and occasionally he took a nip to take the edge off.

Once in the small office, Eddie reached for the whisky and took two big gulps then another one on top. He then sank onto the office desk and just as he did, the phone started ringing and it startled him so much that he started shaking again!

Eddie glanced at the office clock. It was five p.m. It would be Ingrid; of course it would be Ingrid. Who did he think it would be? The corpse of a prostitute?

He pulled himself together in a way which only the thought of Ingrid could enable. Five p.m. on the dot, every evening, if he wasn't back in the house.

Five p.m. every bloody time, for years, for all his married life, a phone call at five p.m. to see where he was.

He used to think it was endearing. He used to think it was because she wanted his tea to be ready for him. What a load of nonsense. This was INGRID. It was just about control.

As the shrill tone of the phone continued ringing, even in the state he was in, Eddie knew he had to answer. If he didn't answer, Ingrid would be round here to see what was keeping him, and the first sight she would see as she came through the door would be a dead body!

Yes, Ingrid would see the dead body of a woman she had never met but had known about, a dead woman nearly twenty years younger than her, who hadn't had a life of privilege and ease.

Eddie knew he couldn't let that happen, so he answered the phone and took another swig of Scotch as he tried to keep his voice steady.

'How long are you going to be, Eddie? Lucy wants to go trick-or-treating, and we haven't got all night.'

'For God's sake, Ingrid, it's the lad's birthday. I'm getting a takeaway.'

The conversation between them was tense.

'Not my problem, Eddie.' Ingrid's voice remained calm, of course. 'I've made my feelings clear! If you're not back in fifteen minutes, the kid will have to come in there with you. Lucy and I are going trick-or-treating, and that's that.'

Eddie sighed, resigned. 'Okay. I will be round in ten minutes. Don't send the lad back in here,' he said and he hung up the phone.

Now Eddie had no choice. 'Face your fears.' He could hear his father's words ringing in his ears. 'Face your fears, or face Ingrid!' He would rather face his fears.

As Eddie took yet another gulp of Scotch, he realised that the bottle was nearly empty. However, he felt calmer with a little bit of Dutch courage inside him. He knew what he had to do, and he knew he had to do it quickly!

Maybe he should be thanking Ingrid – what a thought! But the only thing scaring him more than tending to that corpse out there was the thought of her turning up here and asking questions, or sending the boy back in. That would be disastrous, but maybe that was how the fates had already decided it should be!

As Eddie slowly approached the body bag, coming from a different direction this time, he felt himself start to shake again. He had to brace himself for what was coming, but he had no choice!

It wouldn't take long. He found himself talking out loud for some reason. 'Just move her from the bag to the coffin and that's it. She will be gone tomorrow.'

Eddie took little steps toward the body as if stalling for time, even though he didn't have much of it!

He closed his eyes for the last few steps, until he knew from memory and from holding out his hands to guide him that he was once again standing directly in front of her, his head positioned right above her, and then he opened his eyes slowly, breathing deeply. He looked down at her again.

My God! She was still pretty. She had apparently been dead for weeks, but he could see that she was still pretty.

She still had her nails and teeth intact; not always the case weeks after death!

'There is something healthy about having a relationship with death, how it looks and smells and how it's a transition which we will all experience.'

Eddie found himself quoting comforting words, words which he usually bestowed on grieving families but needed himself at this moment.

Why was he comforting himself, he wondered. Was he grieving? Of course he wasn't grieving; he had hardly known her.

As he prepared himself to lift her slight, cold body from bag to coffin, putting on a face mask and gloves, he knew he was going to feel sick afterwards. This small, pretty woman, now a corpse, had probably only been in her early twenties when he had used her, violated her, paid her for her services, abused the sad, poverty-stricken life she had led.

Heart failure, the priest had said, maybe from living a life of being used and abused, more sexual partners than she was likely to remember – 'clients'. Did that lifestyle contribute to a weak heart? Eddie didn't know ... maybe.

As he removed the body bag from under the corpse, he realised that he didn't even know her name, so before he lifted her into the coffin, he ripped open the paperwork which had been delivered with her.

As he opened it, he realised that no-one had come forward after her death; no-one had identified her. The paperwork referred to her as 'U. P.' (unidentified person), estimated age, thirty-three, taken from dental examination.

As Eddie looked at the paperwork, he realised that he could provide more information about her. He could tell the police where she had lived ten years ago and what she did for a living. Then he realised that they would already know. There would be social security links, bills, and documents in her home, but no-one had formally confirmed who she was or identified her, so she was just a 'U. P.'.

Eddie jumped as the phone in the office started ringing again. He glanced at the clock – ten past five!

'Do it, just do it,' he said to himself. 'Get on with it, and then it will be over!'

He put the paperwork down. He would need to seal and file it, *for what it's bloody worth*, he thought!

Eddie turned his back, as if in slow motion, as if he were standing watching someone else and then he quickly and urgently put his arms under her back and under her head and lifted her easily from the trolley to the coffin.

It took about ten seconds, if that. To Eddie, it felt like a lifetime!

He was excruciatingly aware that this was not the first time in his life that his hands were on this woman's body, touching her flesh, now cold and clammy, previously warm, alive, and inviting! Oh God, yes, she had been inviting.

For the last couple of seconds, as he placed her into the coffin, he fought the urge to just drop her, let her land any way she fell, then close the coffin lid and just run, but he didn't, despite the burning desire to do so, because the shame he felt overwhelmed every other feeling within him. It felt like pure hatred of himself!

He had everything. He had been brought up with love and respect, the word respect running through his mind now, causing him a physical pain in his chest!

He had never known what it must be like to live in poverty, to be hungry, thirsty, cold, unloved – unwanted!

What must it have been like for her to have to sell the only thing she had on offer simply to survive – her body. That was all she had had, her body, which was now lifeless and no good to her any more.

Images of those nights flashed through Eddie's mind. He was sure sex workers had sophisticated ways of advertising themselves these days – 'escorts', later offering their clients 'extras'. But not so for this poor soul. It was word-of-mouth that her grubby little flat was a brothel, and men came and went however they pleased, paying by the hour.

The shame continued to engulf Eddie as he thought back to why he had done it. Okay, Ingrid had fast turned out not to be the woman he had thought she was, and yes, he was lonely and desperate for comfort and sex, but none of that excused him!

He didn't know if he was looking for excuses within his own mind, reasons which would make him feel better, but he told himself that he hadn't set out to use this poor dead woman or to hurt or violate anyone, he really hadn't!

Eddie hadn't planned to use prostitutes in a calculating way. He hadn't gone online looking for sex to purchase. He hadn't thought about it until he had heard some lads in the pub laughing about what they could get for fifty quid in the rundown flats downtown.

The first night it happened, he hadn't left the house with that in mind. He had left the house to get away from Ingrid, to go for a walk, her words ringing in his ears – 'Not a real man' – as he slammed the door behind him.

He hadn't intentionally walked downtown to where the prostitutes hung out, some on the street corners, some in their windows, beckoning, offering, inviting!

He was making excuses for himself. He had headed there, and he took his pick and then he violated this dead woman's body, then he paid her, then he left her in her grubby, cold little flat while he returned home to comfort and warmth, even if it wasn't coming from his wife!

Eddie had returned a few times after that first night. He always headed to the same flat because she knew what he wanted, and she gave it freely. Well, not exactly freely but a bargain!

The shame and regret hit Eddie again. Like a runaway train, it hit him hard, and he vomited as he took a final look at her body, lying dead in front of him!

After Eddie had emptied the contents of his stomach into a bin usually used for the dirty tissues left by grieving friends and relatives, he suddenly knew that he had to do something for her, something to say sorry, something to show his respect for her as a human being and not just a prostitute whose body he had used when it had been alive!

Still feeling sick with shame and guilt, he now knew what he was going to do.

Later, much later, when everyone was asleep, he would come back. He would embalm her to make her look fuller and more alive, he would use filler to plump out her thin lips and now sunken cheeks, he would style her hair and ensure that her scar, where the top of her skull had been removed and put back as part of the postmortem, was concealed, and then he would apply make-up and paint her nails.

Yes, Eddie's mind was made up. She was to have the full package, and she would go to her maker looking the best she could!

He would use all the skills he had. All the training which Ingrid had scoffed at would be put to good use tonight to make this poor soul look serene, peaceful, and respectable ahead of her cremation the next day.

Yes, that's what he would do to say sorry. Eddie was a lonely man, he knew that about himself, but something else, something different to loneliness had died in him today!

In life, he had disrespected her body. In death, he would honour it!

And on that, Eddie closed the coffin lid ... UNTIL LATER, MUCH LATER!

He made his way out of the workshop and back into the kitchen, just as the phone in the office started ringing again!

'Death is not the greatest loss in life,
The greatest loss is what dies inside us while we live.'
(Research)

CHAPTER 9

'WHEN BAD SEEKS REVENGE' –
BLOOD RELATED

Leo couldn't get to sleep. He hadn't experienced this problem for the last few months, not since he had started to feel that Dad had actually wanted him!

Tonight felt strange. Dad and he had shared a Chinese takeaway while Ingrid and Lucy went trick-or-treating – *stupid game, that was*, he thought!

Dad had been distracted tonight. No doubt about it, he didn't want to talk about tomorrow's funeral. Usually, he would share the details of what flowers there were going to be, whether there would be hymns, whether it was a cremation or a burial, but tonight he didn't want to talk about it.

Leo only knew there was going to be a funeral tomorrow because he had been sitting looking out of the window when a van had arrived late, and a body got carried in.

When he had asked Dad about it, he was stand-offish. 'The funeral is tomorrow; just leave it at that,' he had snapped.

No embalming then, thought Leo, no 'titivation'. That was always done the day before!

Leo turned over in bed again, restless, trying to get comfortable. He suddenly realised that he was picking at his hands again. Why was he so on edge tonight? He didn't recognise it as such, of course, but he knew that he just couldn't get to sleep!

Leo misunderstood the reasons for his restlessness, not old enough to understand a sense of foreboding or a gut feeling that something bad was about to happen!

He thought that his newfound dad was losing interest in him already, that he would be unwanted again. How many times could someone not be wanted? As he picked at his hands furiously now, he felt a strong, powerful anger return to him.

'Loneliness and the feeling of being unwanted
is the most terrible poverty.'
(Research – Mother Teresa)

Eddie was trying to pretend that he was asleep as Ingrid got ready for bed. God knew why they still shared a bed, but they did.

God knew why they still shared a house, actually; appearances, he supposed! Ingrid was all about appearances!

Some couples stayed together for the kids. Well, that was a bloody joke in this case. What a complicated mess!

As Ingrid climbed into bed beside him, inches away but worlds apart, Eddie tried to feign deep breathing, as if he were asleep. His body was tense, however, and he tried to relax it, not quite sure why he was bothering.

He was pretty sure that Ingrid couldn't care less whether he was awake, asleep, or dead!

DEAD! The word hit him like a thunderbolt.

That poor woman, lying in the workshop, less than five minutes away. She was dead, and he owed her, he wasn't sure exactly what, but he just felt that he owed her something!

Eddie kept perfectly still as he waited for Ingrid to fall asleep. He kept his breathing level and even, tried to make it sound like a slight snore. He needn't have bothered.

Ingrid was asleep within minutes of getting into bed – a few glasses of wine earlier, Eddie suspected!

Ingrid drank wine on a regular basis. When they were younger, Eddie used to dread it. Some would say, 'It loosened her tongue.'

He would say, 'It made her downright bloody nasty.'

Over the years he had got past caring. It sent her to sleep so that was a bonus, usually a deep sleep which lasted soundly until morning.

He used to resent it, but tonight, more than any other night ever before, he thanked God for it!

> 'Let her sleep … for when she wakes,
> she will shake the world.'
> (Research)

Leo knew how to guess the time accurately without a clock or device. His hypervigilance came from his early years, when he worked out it was about eleven p.m. when the men started arriving – kicking-out time at the pub! The men who came to visit his real mother usually stayed about an hour. That would make it midnight.

Once the men had gone, when he was old enough, he used to help his mum get to bed or get her some water to wash herself. If she had been hurt, sometimes she would just want him to sit by her until she fell asleep.

It hadn't dawned on Leo that she used him for comfort. He didn't understand, but he knew that were many nights when it was often about one a.m. in the morning by the time he slipped back into his bed and felt safe enough to go to sleep!

Leo knew instinctively that it was about one a.m. when he heard Eddie leave his bedroom and make his way downstairs, and he wondered what was going on.

In the year that he had lived there, through the sometimes sleepless nights, especially at the beginning, Leo had *never* known his dad get up and go back downstairs once he had gone to bed for the night.

Leo, yet again, did not understand his own emotions, much less his actions. He had never learned about emotional regulation or behaviour. He had spent his early years simply trying to survive.

He didn't stop to reason why he silently and carefully got out of bed, tiptoed out of his bedroom and followed Eddie downstairs.

He had learned to be sneaky from an early age, and he had practised it when he had secretly watched Eddie do things in the workshop which he wasn't supposed to see, and he very carefully used that sneakiness now!

Leo kept enough distance behind his dad to enable him to hide in the night shadows if Eddie were to turn around unexpectedly. He knew how to be very light-footed, barely making a sound, and he knew which of the stairs and floorboards to avoid because they creaked.

Even his breathing was done with precision, as if he had learned to be invisible all of his life, which, when considered, he probably had been – invisible and unwanted!

Leo felt a rush of adrenalin run through him as he watched Eddie, the only dad he had ever known, take the keys

110

for the workshop from the key stand and move quietly toward the door which led into the adjoining building – the house of the dead!

Surely his dad wasn't going in there in the middle of the night? Leo continued to keep his distance well behind as he watched Eddie carefully and quietly slide the two bolts across and turn the key.

He was! He was! Leo couldn't believe it. His dad was going to go into the workshop, the undertakers, effectively a morgue, IN THE MIDDLE OF THE NIGHT!

Why? Leo wondered. *What could possibly be the reason for that!*

Leo remembered that a 'delivery' had arrived late afternoon, after his dad had sent him back to the house, but it couldn't have anything to do with that. It was very strange. Leo was almost excited at this adventure. The workshop was his favourite place to be!

As Eddie walked from the normality of the family kitchen into the workshop, it dawned on him that he had never entered here in the middle of the night before – why would he? Why would anyone?

He left the adjoining door open. He didn't need to either close or lock it behind him at one fifteen a.m. in the morning.

EDDIE WOULD NEVER GET TO KNOW HOW THAT DECISION SHAPED THE CATASTROPHIC EVENTS WHICH FOLLOWED ...

Had he closed it, it was unlikely that Leo could have opened it without being heard, not in the still of the night!

If Eddie had locked the door, Leo wouldn't have been able to follow him. But he didn't. He had no reason to believe that anyone in the house was even awake, and so he left the door unlocked and ajar to make his return trip back to bed easier.

Eddie knew he would be tired when he had completed what he was setting out to do. He was always tired after embalming, and tonight he would welcome the tiredness afterwards, oh yes, he would, but he still doubted it would be enough to enable him to sleep!

Before he approached the coffin, he decided to get a few sips of Scotch from his office.

'Shit,' he said louder than he should have when he reached the office drawer. There was barely a mouthful left. He must have hammered it earlier.

Leo had just been entering the workshop with the quiet precision of an animal on the hunt when he heard his dad's voice, and it almost caught him off-guard.

He hadn't expected his dad to say anything, let alone shout 'Shit' in the middle of the night. What was going on? He knew that Eddie had gone into the office, but in the dark, he couldn't see anything else.

Leo put his hand out in front of him. He knew the layout well, and his hand was meant to guide him to the curtains and the shelves where the coffins were kept. He knew he could hide and watch from there, so he was surprised to feel something in front of him, something which wasn't usually there and hadn't been there earlier a coffin! There was a coffin in the space which was usually kept free for coming and going!

As his hand touched the shiny wood, almost lovingly, he heard the very faint noise of the coffin handle rattling from the impact.

Leo froze. He didn't know what to do. Surely his dad would have heard that noise from the office? He felt fear, panic, and excitement course through him. He was rooted to the spot and didn't know what to do next!

As Eddie drained the last drop of Scotch from the bottle in his office, he thought he heard a very faint noise in the workshop. Please, God, don't let Ingrid have followed him. Please, God, no, no, not tonight. He wouldn't be able to explain; he couldn't explain. PLEASE, GOD, NO!

He realised that he should turn the office lamp on. That would give enough light for him to see if he had been followed. He did so, almost subconsciously, bracing himself for the possibility that Ingrid might be there. She might have followed him, and she would demand an explanation!

The light from the lamp didn't make a huge impact on the darkness of the workshop, but breathing an enormous sigh of relief, it gave Eddie enough reassurance that Ingrid wasn't there! There was no-one out there other than the poor, frail corpse of the woman, the prostitute that he owed something to!

Eddie didn't know whether to leave the office lamp on or switch it off. He had planned on working by candlelight. He knew what he was doing, after all, and the workshop lights were too bright to put on in the middle of the night without potentially drawing attention through the glass windows which faced directly toward the road out front!

The office lamp, on the contrary, was dim, very dim, but it would provide him with a little bit of extra visibility and couldn't be seen from the front window, so he left it on.

Eddie knew he was wired as he left the office. He headed toward the coffin and tried to compose himself.

This was surreal. He felt as though he were dreaming, but he had to do this. He would get it over with, and then he would put all his memories behind him and get on with his life. He hoped sincerely that he would then feel some peace.

As he approached her body, he decided that he was going to lock the adjoining door after all. Thinking he had heard a noise had rattled him!

If Ingrid did wake and come looking, she would have to go and find the spare keys from the safe before she could get in. That would buy him some time to cover up!

So, Eddie closed and locked the door, the door which for the whole of his adult life had divided the living from the dead, his home from his work, his sad marriage from the sad relatives he comforted, and as he turned the key and set about the task ahead, he was sure that he wouldn't be disturbed. There was only him and the corpse in the room, after all!

So, as Eddie lit the two large table candles he had brought with him to serve the purpose, as he plugged in the embalming machine, unpacked the surgical fillers, prepared the funeral cosmetology and gowned and masked himself, he had no idea at all of the little figure hiding behind a row of unused coffins, breathing quietly, watching his adoptive father's every move as he picked at his hands furiously!

Eddie lifted the coffin lid, nervously this time, because he knew who was lying there, dead, in front of him.

He looked down at her. The shame of what he had done years ago was threatening to engulf him again.

Well, he had no Scotch left, so he might as well get on with it, he thought to himself!

He recoiled slightly at the touch of her. Even though her body had been preserved on ice for weeks, in just the hours which had passed since she had travelled from the hospital morgue and lay there, her body had deteriorated. She was starting to decompose and smell, the smell he knew so well – the smell of death!

Eddie listened to the steady whirr of the embalming machine. It sounded louder than it did during the day, but it was still quiet enough not to be heard or attract any attention, respectfully quiet, Eddie thought – how appropriate!

Eddie felt lightheaded as he picked up the forceps and began the task of draining the blood from her jugular vein in order to inject the formaldehyde, the embalming solution, into her carotid artery with a small tube.

He silently muttered to himself, 'Pull yourself together.' He had performed this task hundreds of times, for God's sake. Just because it was the middle of the night and just because he knew this dead person, well, used to, sort of … His mind was racing. Just get on with it; just get on with it!

It takes about a gallon of embalming solution for every fifty to seventy-five pounds of body weight, and so at least with her being so slight, it wouldn't be as long a job as it could have been, Eddie told himself, as a means of some reassurance.

Leo watched as his dad started acting like a doctor – machine, gown, gloves, instruments … what on earth was he doing!

From the glimpses Leo had stolen before, when Eddie hadn't known he was secretly watching, he knew that his dad 'did things' to the dead bodies to make them look better because he had heard him and Ingrid talk about it. Ingrid usually talked about how much money they made from it!

Leo had never, however, got past the part where his dad started touching the bodies. This was all new, and he realised that he was now shaking. He was, of course, picking at his hands furiously, but he was also somehow very excited. He wanted to see what happened next. He really did want to see what happened next!

Once Eddie had finished draining the blood in order to inject the embalming fluid, he knew the hardest part of all was just about to start. He had to lift her from the coffin and onto the trolley to perform the next bit. He didn't feel as strong in the middle of the night as he did in the day, and for the second time that night, he was thankful that she was of slight bodyweight.

He carefully manoeuvred his hands under her back and under her legs as he set about the task of moving her for the second time today, ensuring as he did that he did not disconnect the machinery.

Eddie again recoiled as he lifted her. He wasn't sure this time whether it was because of the onset of decomposition or other things ... things from the past!

Leo took a sharp intake of breath, louder than he would have wanted, much louder, as he realised that his dad was moving the body, lifting it out of the coffin and placing it onto the trolley which sat waiting.

He wanted to run away now. He didn't want to watch now. He didn't want to be here any more. He had wanted to know all about what his dad did with dead bodies, but now, here in the middle of the night, he DID NOT want to know any more.

It was Halloween; it was his birthday. What his dad did had always intrigued him. He wanted to learn everything, had crept around and hidden when he could, just to watch, but he suddenly wanted to be anywhere but here!

Leo knew there was nowhere to go, no escape. He had seen Eddie lock the door between here and the kitchen, and so there was nowhere to go without revealing himself.

Leo decided that he wouldn't look, decided that he wasn't as interested as he had thought he was in undertakers and dead bodies and what went on between them! He wished he were back in bed!

As Eddie lay her body on the trolley and gently and methodically set about the injection process, he somehow managed to go into 'work mode' and started to perform the task the same as he had done hundreds of times before … in the day … on corpses he didn't know!

Yes, he was still shaky, still unnerved by the whole situation, but somehow, he had found a way to focus and do what he knew he had to do.

Leo continued to tell himself that he wasn't going to look. He buried his head in his hands and thought ahead. His dad would finish whatever it was he was doing and then he would go to bed, and he, Leo, would be locked in here with a dead body, and then God knew what would happen in the morning when he didn't turn up for breakfast!

Leo couldn't recognise that he was experiencing trauma. He didn't really understand that for the whole of his young life he had been let down by the adults around him. Neglected, hungry, frightened, dismissed by professionals … unwanted, unwanted, unwanted!

Now, here was this further trauma, and he buried his head into his hands, still being as quiet as he could, still the little boy who was shut away in a cupboard when the men came and went and when his mum got hurt.

He didn't realise that he was in turmoil. What he did recognise, however, was the feeling of power which strangely came over him, because actually, although he felt alone and scared, guilty that he had followed his dad in here tonight and scared of the consequences that might bring, he also felt sure that Eddie should not be in here either, not in the middle of the night, not with a dead body!

Leo could not stand Ingrid, *his mother,* not any more than she could stand him. He didn't understand the concept of adult–child relationships. He didn't know adults were supposed to look after and protect children. He thought it was an even playing field!

He thought more about Ingrid and wondered what she would do if she knew Eddie was here in the dead of the night, working on a corpse!

Leo knew there was something wrong with this situation. He was scared, but he was tingling, excited, and felt a strange sense of power about the whole thing.

Somehow, Leo knew, without really knowing, that this was not going to end well!

He did not know how long he had been holding his head in his hands for. He didn't know the time and couldn't even guess it now. He could hear Eddie working on the body, making small sighs from time to time, moving instruments, lifting them up and then putting them back down, and he was sure at one point he heard a hair-dryer being used!

WHAT HAPPENED NEXT SEEMED TO BE IN SLOW MOTION TO LEO. One minute he had his head down, determined not to look at what his dad was doing, and in the next instant he decided to think about taking a look and trying to work out how long his dad was likely to be and how he was going to get out of here and back to bed.

As Leo lifted his head and opened his eyes against the dark, anyone watching may have thought that it was a sheer fluke or stroke of bad luck for him that the moon lingered directly over the small window which sat in the roof. This enhanced the dim light from the office and also assisted the two candles, which had now burned half way down.

This fluke or stroke of bad luck left Leo in a position to see clearly the face of the corpse, which by now Eddie was powdering and adding blusher to.

A VERY YOUNG LIFETIME OF MEMORIES SUDDENLY HIT AND FLOODED LEO TO THE VERY CORE – PAINFUL, MISERABLE, SORROWFUL MEMORIES!

The woman … the body … the corpse. She had been the cause of his suffering. She had never loved him, never wanted him, gave him away to a FUCKING FOREVER FAMILY!

The woman … the body … the corpse … HIS MOTHER!

Leo didn't realise that he had lunged forward. It happened instinctively, before he thought about it!

He was beside the corpse now, beside his MOTHER … HIS REAL MOTHER … HIS DEAD MOTHER …

He looked down at her. She actually looked better dead than she had ever looked when she was alive!

Drugs and alcohol had ravished her looks when she lived, despite her being naturally pretty.

Now, however, her face looked fuller and calmer than in life. She was tastefully presented with subtle make-up and styled hair, thanks to the skills of his 'DAD', Leo thought scathingly!

LEO POUNCED, not like a young boy in shock or distress but like an animal which had been caged for years and was suddenly let free. He ran at his 'DAD' like something wild and dangerous!

As his body connected with Eddie's, Leo clawed at Eddie's face. His neglected fingernails were long, and the contact drew blood.

Then he felt himself biting; what was he biting? He thought briefly, with no real interest, was it a nose or a cheek? He didn't care. Vague memories of someone biting him a long time ago slipped into his mind. He didn't know if it was his memory or imagination. He recalled a man, once, a long time ago, when he had tried to protect his mum from a beating!

Leo was ferocious now, scratching, biting, limbs flaying around as he tried his hardest to cause hurt and pain. Oh yes, he knew all about hurt and pain!

Eddie went into shock. One minute he had almost completed the task he had set out to do, a good task in his opinion – amends! But just as he had started to feel the relief of knowing it was nearly over, he found himself being attacked.

He didn't realise to begin with that his attacker was Leo. The workshop was not well lit purposely. However, the moon had settled over the Skylark, which had added some extra light and vision.

When a figure came lunging toward Eddie from the dark, his first thought was, *Ingrid*. He wasn't really thinking straight and wasn't therefore thinking logically. He didn't grasp immediately that the little person lunging himself at him, scratching and biting, was far too small to be Ingrid. His mind was on autopilot. Who else in the world would want to attack him, other than his shrew of a wife if she caught him embalming a prostitute in the middle of the night!

Neither did it dawn on Eddie that he had locked the door before starting his work, and he hadn't heard it being opened.

After about sixty seconds, maybe it was a bit longer, Eddie suddenly realised that it was Leo who was clinging to him, attacking him, biting and scratching him. The realisation made him go numb. He didn't know what to do. Leo was like a clinging monkey which wouldn't let go, but his actions were more venomous than any monkey. He was completely vicious. Eddie could feel blood running down his cheeks and face where Leo had bitten and scratched him.

Eddie tried to get the boy off him. Ingrid's words were now ringing in his ears. God, she was right, Leo was a feral brat. The kid had gone mad, lost his senses. How the hell had he got in here!

Eddie thought back to the slight noise he had heard earlier, the noise which had spooked him a bit. God! The boy must have followed him in here before he locked the door, must have watched the whole thing!

Leo suddenly went limp, and Eddie seized his chance to fling him away. Leo stumbled backwards and would likely have fallen flat on his back if it weren't for the trolley where the corpse lay … where his MOTHER lay!

Neither Eddie nor Leo said anything initially. They couldn't find words, and both were out of breath and panting. Shocked and trembling, they looked at each other after what seemed like a lifetime of silence.

They both vied the other as though they were seeing each other for the first time.

After moments of silence and panting, moments of 'father' and 'son' staring at each other, it was Leo who spoke first, and Eddie could not believe what he was hearing. In a man's voice, nothing like that of a nine-year-old child, Leo growled, 'That's my MOTHER!'

Eddie faltered. He had been about to say, 'Why are you here? Why have you followed me? What the hell are you doing?'

But instead, he said, 'What did you say?'

Leo, slowly, calmly now, but still in a voice far too old for his age, repeated himself. 'I said, that's my MOTHER!' and he turned to look directly at his mother's corpse!

Eddie couldn't speak; he couldn't respond. He opened his mouth to say something, but no words came out.

Leo stood looking at the dead body of his mother, his *real* mother, for a while, and then he once again addressed Eddie, still in an adult tone. 'Why are you here in the middle of the night with my MOTHER's body?'

Eddie was further thrown into some type of confusion and bewilderment. Maybe this was a bad dream!

'WHAT WERE YOU DOING TO MY MOTHER?' Leo repeated, louder now, more agitated again!

For the first time, notwithstanding the shock of everything which was going on, Eddie started to feel scared, very scared! Leo was calm, calmer than he had probably ever been in his sad and neglected life. He felt in control all of a sudden. He couldn't understand his emotions, he never could, but he now felt the most engulfing power, and along with it he felt something else bubbling … he wanted REVENGE! Oh God, yes, he wanted REVENGE!

He wanted REVENGE for the fact that he had been born a bastard!

He wanted REVENGE for the miserable early days of neglect and poverty!

He wanted REVENGE for a mother who had never wanted him but now lay here dead!

He wanted REVENGE for being adopted into a family who never wanted him either!

Much to Eddie's horror, Leo moved toward the trolley where the corpse lay. Eddie didn't know what to expect next. He wanted to be out of here, God, yes, he wanted to be a long way away from here, anywhere, as long as it was a long, long way away from this workshop, this corpse, this complex and dangerous child!

As Leo looked down at his mother's corpse, the woman who for seven years of his life had maybe tried her best, he wasn't sure where his growing anger was placed.

Was it all her fault? Why didn't she try harder to keep him, to love him like other mothers did? Even Ingrid cherished her own kid!

Leo was trembling again, not just a shudder or a shiver but uncontrollable trembling all over.

His mother looked well. He sniggered at this thought. She looked ... *well* ... not black and blue, not plastered in thick make-up as a cover up. Her hair was clean, and she looked peaceful. He had never seen her look peaceful in her life, always nervy, always agitated, or silly and tearful after she had been drinking from the boozy bottle.

Leo could not take his eyes off her, and for about five minutes he stood there. It would have looked a very strange sight for anyone looking on, but of course there was no-one else, just Leo, a small boy, still shaking, picking at his hands again, looking down at the dead body of a woman on a trolley, being watched carefully by a very nervous Eddie, a large, cumbersome man, who now looked very vulnerable with his unbelieving expression and blood dripping down his face.

Leo didn't know what to do next. He wanted to carry on lashing out, make someone pay for the miserable existence which other kids called a life.

Thoughts were swimming through his head. How did she die? How did she end up here? Why was Eddie working on her body in the middle of the night?

The situation seemed to go full circle, and Leo again boomed at Eddie, 'WHAT WERE YOU DOING TO MY MOTHER?' Eddie was defeated, he was in shock, he knew nothing could ever be the same after tonight. The boy would have to go back, then he would confess to Ingrid, and then he would ask for a divorce. He would have to take his chances maintaining a relationship with Lucy. This was it, a game changer. Life was going be different after tonight!

Eddie didn't realise that in his shock he was method-ically planning his future in his mind. Neither did he comprehend that when he answered Leo, it was how he would have responded to an adult and not how he should have responded to a child.

'I was preparing her for her funeral tomorrow,' he said.

'In the middle of the fuckin' night?' Leo questioned menacingly.

'I didn't have time to do it today.' Eddie continued,

'She arrived late, and you know what a stickler your mother is if I don't finish work at five.'

Leo's anger was almost overspilling again now. 'Ingrid is NOT my fuckin' MOTHER. *This* is MY MOTHER, lying here dead, on YOUR trolley, in the middle of the FUCKIN' night.

Did you know her?' Leo remained menacing. 'I used to,' said Eddie honestly but clumsily, and he soon real-ised his mistake.

'You used to know her ... you used to know her?' Leo was looking at Eddie as if he were trying to work some-thing out, but he didn't know what!

'It was a long time ago,' said Eddie, making it worse!

Leo once again sprang forward onto Eddie, clinging like a leech. The trolley holding the corpse of his mother rolled away from him as he once again bit and scratched Eddie like a wild ravaged animal!

'You BASTARD! YOU fuckin' BASTARD! They call *me* that name, but YOU are the BASTARD, NOT ME! You were one of the men, weren't you? One of the men who hurt her and beat her black and blue?'

Eddie was trying to un-grip Leo's hands from where they had once again sunk into him, his neck this time, trying desperately to get the boy's legs from around him!

125

He was breathless as he panted, 'I never hurt your mother, never. I only met her a couple of times. It must have been long before you were born.'

Leo had now lost all control. His senses were devoid as he carried on scratching and biting, clinging to Eddie until he realised what he was going to do.

'I AM GOING TO KILL YOU!' He spat the words out. 'I AM GOING TO FUCKIN' KILL YOU!'

Eddie knew it was time to try and get help. Leo's anger, his words, they weren't enough to alert anyone, not in here with the door locked and just a bit of light!

If he could get the boy off him, he could throw something heavy through the window to gain attention. Something instinctively told Eddie that the boy was capable of killing him.

Eddie couldn't rationalise that Leo had obviously had an enormous shock seeing his dead mother's body – no! His self-preservation came above that thought, and he just knew he was fighting for his life!

As Leo continued to scratch and bite him with no sign of getting tired or letting go, Eddie's eyes scanned the room for something to throw. It would need to be something heavy – the glass was strengthened.

Eddie was starting to feel weak. The boy was still clinging onto him, no sign of letting up!

He didn't know how long this went on for until he first realised that blood was running down his chest and arms, much more blood than could be possible from scratches and bites!

Eddie was feeling very weak now – faint! Leo had let go and was standing in front of him looking shocked and dazed, tired at last!

Eddie could feel a throbbing pain in the side of his neck. His mind was all confused. There was a lot of blood. Where had all the blood come from? Eddie fell to his knees, unable to stay upright. His legs just crumpled, and he thought he was going to lose consciousness.

As Eddie slipped clumsily to the floor, half-aware he was sliding down and half-unable to comprehend what was happening, he saw it! He saw the TROCAR, the long needle, lying on the floor. It had blood on it and around it. Leo was quiet now, standing before Eddie, looking down at him, appearing in shock himself!

Realisation started to hit Eddie as he managed to raise his hand and touch his neck. LEO HAD STABBED HIM! THE BOY HAD STABBED HIM WITH HIS OWN TROCAR, the very same needle Eddie had used to drain the corpse's body before he embalmed her!

He always cleaned his instruments as he went along, as he worked – he prided himself on it! The Trocar had been clean, clean and sterilised, and now it was covered in blood ... his blood ... his own blood! As Eddie felt the wound, just as he was losing consciousness, he wasn't really registering the pain. It felt more like a dull pulsing sensation, as if someone were gently tapping him!

Eddie knew from feeling the wound that he had been stabbed in the carotid artery. Only doctors or undertakers were likely to have this awareness, he thought cynically as unconsciousness really started to overpower him!

He knew the blood supply to his brain was being affected. His life flashed before him as he slipped further and further away!

A happy childhood, mapped out for him in many ways, groomed into the family business, respectable, easygoing.

Then meeting Ingrid, how it all went wrong, the desperation for a child, the happiness of Lucy, then the adoption!

As Eddie finally slipped into an unconsciousness which he would never recover from, his penultimate thought was that he had decided tonight to sort his life out, to get a divorce and find peace – TOO LATE!

His final thoughts, however, were about Leo, the boy standing before him now, white and pale, small again, shaking, picking his hands and looking scared and vulnerable, no anger now, no adult voice or bad language.

The boy must be a psychopath, and yet there had been a bond there. Eddie had taken to the boy for a while, considered him his own.

So, Ingrid had been right. He should have listened to her this time, like he had always listened to her before. The boy was feral, bad, likely from bad blood!

As Eddie's life slipped away, there was nothing anyone could have done for him. His body lay on the stone-cold floor of his own undertaker's workshop, blood still dripping from his neck initially and then slowly stopping as the life ebbed out of him!

Eddie, the undertaker, salt of the earth, pillar of the community, the priest had thought the day before, dead on the floor less than two feet away from the corpse of a young unidentified woman while a young boy looked on helplessly as he realised what he had done!

'I am a child, with nothing left, with nothing more to give,
There's only so much one can take, but I am going to live,
I have no conscience any more, I know that will be said,
I can be good ... but also bad, and someone ends up dead.'

CHAPTER 10

'FOREVER BAD' – THE FINAL LABEL

'My God, that's one fucked up kid,' the sergeant managing the case muttered to himself.

He could not quite believe this case, the strangeness and the complexities within it!

The police who had arrived at the scene, two of them, were both in shock!

The call had come in at about six fifteen a.m., a hysterical woman screeching that her life was in danger. The call didn't make any sense until officers arrived at the scene.

'I've just woken up and couldn't find my husband …' The first sentence was coherent but after that the woman was chaotic. 'I found him in the workshop … on the floor, covered in blood … there's another corpse in there as well. It wasn't there earlier … The boy, the monster, he used the Trocar to drain his blood. He's still in there, rocking back and forth … He's evil, possessed, he'll kill Lucy and me … HELP! HELP!'

When the officers arrived at the scene, the woman's words did fall into place, although they couldn't grasp the enormity of the crime scene and called for backup immediately.

The woman who had rung, the funeral director's wife, was in the kitchen with a young female child. The door between the kitchen and the funeral parlour was locked and bolted, and the woman told the officers that she feared for their lives. 'The evil child is in the workshop!'

The female officer tried to console the hysterical woman and comfort the child, who sat beside her looking bemused.

Once support arrived, the male officer took the keys from the table and unlocked the door which led through to the funeral parlour, or the workshop, as it was commonly known!

As he and four back-up officers pushed open the door, they did not know what to expect – was the woman mad! Had she lost her mind! Were they going to find something gruesome on the other side of the door!

In his heart, the officer, who had thirty years' service under this belt, knew that they were going to be facing something bad. His senses were tingling, and the very core of his instinct was warning him to be prepared for the worst!

Nothing, however, could have prepared him for the sight he found before him as he tentatively entered the cold and still dimly lit workshop.

His eyes widened as he first caught a glance of the corpse on the trolley! A dead woman just lying there, motionless, make-up and hair all fresh, like an oversized doll just left in the middle of nowhere!

Behind the corpse, on the floor, lay a man, a large man. There was dried blood all around his neck and body and on the floor. His face was white and ghostly, and the officer couldn't actually tell if he was dead or alive!

But it was the third thing the officer saw which caused him the most anxiety – a boy, a little boy, a child sitting beside the man while reaching out, also touching the woman's corpse and just rocking backwards and forwards, moaning in a low tone like a wounded animal might!

As the back-up officers started immediately sealing off the scene and calling for forensics and ambulances, the officer called to his female colleague, who had remained in the kitchen. This kid needed a woman to help him.

As his colleague joined him at the scene, he could see the shock and horror on her face at the sight of the corpse, the bloody body, and the boy. She gasped and tried to compose herself. Did she imagine that the corpse of the woman looked vaguely familiar? However, the line of duty called, and so she clumsily made her way to the child!

Leo looked up, startled, as she moved towards him. He didn't know what to expect. As she got close to him, he thought he recognised her. Yes, it was, it was her, the pleasant round-faced lady who had been kind to him that night when the police came to his old house, the flat with the cupboard, the night his real mum had said she had never wanted him, the night his journey into adoption began, when being unwanted all over again was only just starting.

It seemed a lifetime ago. He was only nine years old. It had been two years since then. Everything was a blur. Maybe everything had all been a bad dream, and he would wake up in the cupboard under the stairs and his mum would be black and blue!

He wasn't sure what was real and what wasn't real any more. However, two very real dead bodies told him that this was NO nightmare which he would wake up from!

As the kindly policewoman knelt beside him, she put her hand calmly on his arm. 'It's Leo, isn't it?' she said kindly!

Leo gave her a little nod as he continued to rock and moan. He removed his hand from his mother's corpse now and started picking at it ... picking ... picking ... picking ... unwanted ... unwanted ... unwanted!

Jesus Christ, thought the officer, *what the hell was this child doing here in the middle of all this carnage? WHAT THE HELL!* She did, however, go into autopilot and found a blanket to wrap around him, as he was shivering, and she spoke to him in very gentle and quiet terms, just like the last time they had met!

The last time, God, the last time, Halloween, two years ago, she had led him away to social workers with the hope that he might find a happy ending!

She was sure someone had mentioned him since and said they had found a nice adoptive home for him!

As she led him away this time, to the emergency social workers, AGAIN, she was sure he would not be going anywhere nice if the scene which surrounded him had anything to do with him. What a bloody mess!

She shivered herself as she put her arms around Leo for the second time in his young life. She tried to steady him again as he stumbled along beside her. GOD, SHE HATED THIS FUCKING JOB SOMETIMES!

The sergeant also went into autopilot as the child arrived at the juvenile custody suite.

Arrange a specialist solicitor ...

Arrange an appropriate adult to be with him for his interview ... it would have to be a social worker ... the kid had no one else that was known ...

Search the database for any blood relatives – NOT anyone connected to the adopters ...

From first impressions from the scene, from the officers who found the child, then the specialists, then the forensic experts, came the hypothesis that the kid had killed the undertaker, drained the blood from his carotid artery with his, the undertaker's, own instruments!

The scene had been manic, the undertaker's wife screeching and wailing and needing sedation!

The little girl bemused, shocked, a little bit emotionless!

It took the specialist teams longer than usual to piece together the early events, and the full investigation was to follow!

It had been a long few days, and as the sergeant was about to go home for the night to a nice stiff drink and the hope of some sleep, one of the officers called him back.

What now? he thought, and he knew he could have carried on walking. After a twenty-two-hour shift, watching that tiny boy being interrogated, the emotional drain of the whole thing, he knew he could have ignored the officer and carried on walking right out of the station and home, but he didn't!

'Sarge,' said the officer, 'the murdered undertaker case – the DNA is back!'

The sergeant groaned. 'THE MURDERED UNDERTAKER'. God, the press had soon got hold of that one, hadn't they? 'NINE-YEAR-OLD KID DRAINS BLOOD FROM HIS ADOPTIVE FATHER'. The child would never get a fair trial!

The sergeant realised how tired he was as he said, 'DNA isn't likely to be a big factor in this matter, Officer.' His patience was thin!

'The kid was adopted – no DNA match expected.'

The alert young police officer, newly trained, looked at the sergeant, who looked tired and weary! He supposed that's what years of doing this job did to you!

'I don't think you understand, Sarge,' he said. 'There's been a development.

The kid was with his parents at the time of the murder,' said the young officer enthusiastically.

The sergeant groaned. These young, vibrant officers could be great, full of ambition and passion, a breath of fresh air, even, BUT sometimes, they didn't listen, sometimes they let their emotions run away in a genuine bid to 'solve the crime'!

'We know that, Officer,' said the sarge wearily. Once an adoption order was made, the adopters become the legal parents, so yes, Leo was with his parents that night, his legal parents!

'No, no, no,' said the officer almost hyperactively, 'you don't understand – LEO WAS WITH HIS BIOLOGICAL PARENTS THAT NIGHT!'

'What?' said the sarge, convinced now that he definitely needed to get some sleep!

'The corpse, the woman, the unidentified one – she's the kid's mother. She's Leo's biological mother.' Died of natural causes!

'WHAT!' the sarge said loudly but only to himself.

Again, he thought, *everything about this case is fucked up!*

'The kid was removed from his natural mother two years ago, on Halloween, actually. This team dealt with it.' The sergeant sounded bemused.

'Well, DNA doesn't lie, does it, Sarge?' said the officer. The corpse was the kid's mother!

'Okay,' said the sergeant, 'there must be more to this than we know.'

'Leo wasn't just an unwanted kid, then, taking his anger and trauma out on his adoptive father. His mother was in the picture … but dead!' It was getting very complicated!

The officer wasn't excited this time. He was deadly serious as he shared his next piece of information with his senior. Quietly now he said, 'The undertaker wasn't his adoptive father, Sarge. Well, I mean, he was, but that's not all. THE UNDERTAKER WAS LEO'S BIOLOGICAL FATHER!'

TWO DNA EXPERT OPINIONS CAN'T BE WRONG!

The sergeant felt as though he couldn't comprehend or digest any more information. What the fuck? This was impossible. Well, NO, not impossible, but how improbable?

The whole thing made no sense. This was going to be one hell of an investigation!

Not so tired now, the sergeant decided to call in on the juvenile custody suite before he headed home.

Leo was sitting on the floor, close to a cupboard, despite there being comfortable furniture available.

He looked up as the sergeant entered the cell. They called it a 'room' because he was only nine years old, but really it was a cell!

The sergeant noted how small and thin Leo was for his age.

'You've been through it, haven't you, lad?' he said kindly.

Leo didn't answer. He looked down, picking furiously at his hands. He had been the centre of attention since he had arrived. He had been spoken to by social workers, therapists, psychologists, psychiatrists, solicitors, advocates, oh, and of course the police, the police, who wanted to charge him with Eddie's murder!

He hadn't spoken to a single one of them, but he had listened. Oh yes, he had listened to their words, some of which he had heard before, some which were new.

NEGLECTED, SAD, SCARED, PAIN, LONELINESS, RESENTMENT, ANGER … OH, AND REVENGE … LET'S NOT FORGET REVENGE!

Leo was pretty sure that it had been revenge which had made him plunge that instrument into Eddie's neck. It was all so vague now. Eddie was trying to get him off. Leo wanted to carry on biting and scratching, and he wanted to hurt … he wanted to hurt Eddie for all the times men like him had hurt his mother … black and blue!

But these idiots thought he had purposely drained the blood from Eddie's neck because of what he did. Well, it showed how much they know, but he didn't care, anyway. They could think what they liked, swarming around him, and he was all over the papers, not named because of his age, but he knew who he was, and he smiled a little knowing smile – NOT SO UNWANTED NOW!

The sergeant tried to talk to Leo again, but he knew that he would not talk to him. What an investigation this was going to be! What a story. What now for the boy?

The boy, Leo, such a young child, a life ruined before it had even started, nine years old, caught up in a story of neglect, poverty, adoption, intrigue, and MURDER!

His life from now on would be juvenile detention, headlines, blame, shame, and judgement!

What had really happened on that night, on Halloween, in the funeral parlour? The sergeant wondered, all tense and thoughtful now, not tired any more!

Jesus Christ, he was just a kid. What the hell had been happening to him for him to commit such a crime? There would be speculation about abuse, of course there would be. His ADOPTIVE father and him. No, CORRECTION – his BIOLOGICAL father and him, together in the middle of the night in a funeral parlour, in the dark, with the corpse of his mother present!

Leo had been a quiet kid by all accounts even before this, compliant, nervous, even. Well, God help him now!

Leo remained silent as the investigation continued and the trial loomed. He would not give a plea, even with advice, support, and advocacy, so the matter had to go to trial.

He continued to listen to the professionals who were working with him. They were not very bright, Leo had decided. Just because he didn't speak, they must have thought he couldn't hear either – idiots!

Leo heard them all right. 'He's got every God-damned reporter in the land desperate to talk to him, crackpots, pretending to be his real mother ... members of the public, putting themselves on social media saying they know him!'

Oh yes, Leo listened and took it all in, silently. Sometimes, he was still angry, sometimes despondent, sometimes he still felt full of power. But most of the time, he felt like a nine-year-old boy whom nobody had ever wanted!

Sometimes he felt like he was back in the cupboard, listening for the men to come and go, listening for the screams of his mother, his real mother ... black and blue!

But he wasn't back in the cupboard. No, he was in a comfortable CELL, with toys and a clean bed, and everyone wanted to talk to the psychopath kid who had drained his father of blood and murdered him.

Yet he remained silent as they came and went, the same fuckin' professionals who had left him at home with his 'no-hoper' of a mother for seven years ... Prostitute, hooker, whore!

The same fuckin' professionals who thought it would be a GREAT idea to find him a 'forever family to love and cherish him'!

The same fuckin' professionals who visited him for months at Eddie and Ingrid's house and *thought* everything was going great! Successful adoption – CASE CLOSED!

Leo had no intention of telling them anything. Oh yes, they had taken him around the court, showed him where he would be seen through video link as he gave evidence. WHAT A FUCKIN' JOKE. There would be NO evidence from him – 'selectively mute', they said. Well, he would stay that way!

Let them work it out for themselves. Let them make their judgment, and let the judge and jury decide which of the three options they would choose.

WAS HE GOOD?

WAS HE BAD?

WAS HE SIMPLY UNWANTED?

'I am a child who learned to fight, to savage and destroy,
    I used to be a quiet child, the perfect little boy,
I am a child who took revenge, why bother being kind?
A vicious child, a feral child, that's how I'll be defined.
 So, as I sit in my lonely cell, a child alone once more,
    There's a lesson for the lot of you, YOU SHOULD
                    HAVE LOVED ME MORE.'

'Attachment theory is a psychological evolutionary and ethological theory concerning relationships between humans. The most important tenet is that young children need to develop a relationship with at least one primary care giver, for normal social and emotional development.

If you take a new plant and place it in some fertiliser, if you feed and water it regularly, dust it with leaf shine occasionally and place it in the sunlight ... IT WILL THRIVE!

If you take the same plant and place it in a pot of gravel, if you water it with battery acid, tear the leaves and keep it in a cupboard in the dark, it will struggle to cope. It will be a shadow of the plant it might have been if it had been cared for properly.

Children are the same. With the right care, they will do well and have every chance of fulfilling their potential.

But if they are not responded to sensitively, consistently, and with affection, they will adapt to cope as best they can.

These adaptations may look like poor behaviour of different kinds, but in the context of a threat, anger, or neglect, survival takes over, and they of course show up badly.

Such children need to be supported to re-adapt their behaviour, no matter how bad it seems,

They certainly don't, in most cases, need to be punished!'

THOUGHT-PROVOKING QUESTIONS

– Why did Leo's birth mum have tears in her eyes when she said she had never wanted him?
– Why did Leo find comfort in cupboards?
– Did Ingrid and Eddie start out with the right intentions when deciding to adopt a child?
– What made Leo pick his hands?
– Why did Leo sometimes call Eddie by his name and sometimes call him Dad?
– Why did Eddie sometimes call Leo by his name and sometimes call him 'the boy'?
– Why did Leo have a period of stability when he lived with his foster carers?
– What more could the social workers have done?
– Why did Leo enjoy the feeling of power?
– Why did Leo want revenge?

COMING SOON, THE SEQUEL – *The Lonely Kid on Parole*

A HEART FOR AUTHORS À L'ÉCOUTE DES AUTEURS MIA KA
FÖR FÖRFATTARE UN CORAZÓN POR LOS AUTORES YAZARLARIMIZA GÖNÜ
PER AUTORI ET HJERTE FOR FORFATTERE EEN HART VOOR SCHRIJVERS TE
SERCE DLA AUTORÓW EIN HERZ FÜR AUTOREN A HEART FOR AUTH
ВСЕЙ ДУШОЙ К АВТОРАМ ETT HJÄRTA FÖR FÖRFATTARE Á LA ESCUCHA
MIA ΚΑΡΔΙΆ ΓΙΑ ΣΥΓΓΡΑΦΕΙΣ UN CUORE PER AUTORI ET HJERTE FOR FORF
RZÖINKÉRT SERCE DLA AUTORÓW
ΡΑÇÃO ВСЕЙ ДУШОЙ К АВТОРАМ ET

The author

Despite her strong Irish heritage, Diana Jo was born in the West Midlands of England in the early 1960s. The region, known as the 'Black Country' since the mid-nineteenth century due to its numerous ironworking foundries, shaped her upbringing. Today, she resides in Cornwall, fulfilling her lifelong dream of living by the sea. For thirty years, Diana Jo has worked tirelessly as a children's social worker, also fostering many children. Her personal journey through childhood and adolescence gave her strength but also led to introspection into the complexities of human nature. She learned to discern the inherent good and bad in everyone, pondering the fine line between the two.

The main character of her book, Leo, represents a blend of real-life children Diana Jo has encountered and cared for. He embodies aspects of a foster child she once nurtured, a troubled youth she advocated for, and possibly reflections of her own experiences – good, bad, unwanted.

The publisher

He who stops
getting better
stops being good.